BEAR

GUARDIAN DEFENDER

BOOK EIGHT

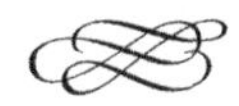

KRIS MICHAELS

Created with Vellum

CHAPTER 1

Bear McGowen flipped his blinker on and exited off Interstate 12 into Baton Rouge. He'd driven from New Orleans, where he'd rented a car after flying into Louis Armstrong. He needed the drive, using the time to let his life as a business owner slip away as he assumed the mantle of a Guardian operative.

The phone call he'd received yesterday was strange, and Bear wasn't sure what he was getting into. The thought that Christopher Whitehead was missing didn't compute, and there were too many holes in his sister's story to provide adequate background to do much of anything, so he decided to travel to Baton Rouge to determine what was happening.

Topher, as he called him, was a friend, albeit one he hadn't talked with much lately. A text here and there after the mission in Cuba had kept them in touch. A nuclear physicist, Topher was one of those people Bear liked straight off the bat. He'd known the instant he saw Topher in Cuba that the man was his mission. Topher was so far out of his element. And indeed, Bear had made sure Whitehead got out of Cuba alive. Thankfully, they all had. Sage Browning, who was now Bear's boss, had been shot but recovered. That mission was a mess of crossed wires and a political quagmire. Thank God Guardian had high cover for all the operatives who infiltrated Cuba to find the dirty bombs, which was why Topher was even on that mission.

As the GPS directed him to Topher's apartment, Bear went over his conversation with Piper Whitehead.

"What?"

"Ah ..." a soft female voice stammered on the other side of the line. "I'm looking for Mr. McGowen."

"I don't want to buy anything," Bear snapped. It was the fifth or sixth time this number had called him without leaving a message. He was over the game. Rude

wasn't his style, but neither was being a pest, which was what he'd labeled the caller. Capital P.

"I'm not selling anything. I'm calling because I think something happened to my brother."

Bear's opinion of the caller shifted, and so did his curiosity. "Who's your brother?"

"Christopher Whitehead. He said if something happened to call you." The words were rushed, and the woman sounded desperate.

Bear's body tightened; his attention focused on the caller at the other end of the line. He leaned forward. "You have my complete attention." Because he knew for a fact that Topher didn't have a family anymore. His mom had passed, and his father had ghosted when Topher was a kid.

"I was gone for three months. I went on a sabbatical, and when I got back, he was gone."

Bear got up, walked to his office door, and closed it. The sounds of the gym, which were usually a comfort, weren't welcome in the conversation. "You'll excuse me if I have trouble with your call. Topher doesn't have any family."

"He didn't. His mom is dead, and his father married my mom. I didn't know he existed. We met at a conference. I'm his half-sister. He convinced me to move down to Baton Rouge from the Univer-

sity of Michigan, so we could work together at LSU."

"And your name is?" Bear wouldn't randomly accept some woman's rattling explanation without verification.

"Piper Whitehead. Please, I know something is wrong. Christopher said he would be here when I got back. He's never lied to me."

"Have you called his cell? Been to his house? His office?" Bear mentioned the normal things a person would have done before calling the cops.

"I have."

"And why haven't you called the police?" He wasn't sold on the woman's story.

"He told me if something happened to him, I was supposed to call you, not the police. He was adamant about that."

"Why would something happen to him?"

"I don't know. Maybe the project he was working on."

"Huh. Okay. Piper, was it?"

"Yes."

"Well, I'm going to do some checking. I'll call you back."

"You'll help?" Her tone shifted from worried to hopeful.

"I'll see what I can do. I'll call you back."

"Thank you."

BEAR STOPPED in a crush of traffic as he waited for the lights to change. His phone rang, and he glanced at the screen to ascertain who it was before he answered. "McGowen."

"Okay, I've got the information you need," Sage, his newly minted boss, said. "Luckily, my lady works from home and doesn't mind doing her soon to be husband a favor. Are you prepared to copy, or do you need me to send this via email after the brief?"

"Send, please. I'm sitting in the middle of rush hour traffic in Baton Rouge."

"Ah, my neck of the woods. I'm not far away if you need help. A couple of hours by truck. But here it goes. Piper Whitehead is, in fact, Christopher's half-sister. She was enrolled in the University of Michigan's master's program but transferred to Louisiana State University and is now enrolled in their doctoral program. Christopher is listed as a tenured professor at LSU."

Bear nodded. So, that part of the woman's story checked out. "All right. If I can get through this traffic, I'll meet with her at his apartment."

"I've up-channeled the possibility that he could be missing simply because of his background."

Bear grunted. "Nuclear physicist? Yeah, I'd say that could be of interest."

Sage made a sound of agreement. "Well, he consulted for the US government's Nuclear Program and the Nuclear Regulatory Commission."

"How did you know that?" Bear had spent plenty of downtime talking with Whitehead in Cuba. Topher never told him anything like that.

"I was on that ship forever while you were drinking Mai Tais on the beach in Cuba."

Bear's laugh was immediate and rang through the SUV. "Fuck you, man."

"Nah, not in the mood. But while I was on the ship, I found everyone's jacket. I read them. Sue me. I was bored."

Well, hell, that made sense. He would have read the files, too. "What's the brass saying?"

"Curious as to what you find. As of about an hour ago, you're assigned to this case. I'll be your POC and backup if you need it. Should this turn into a shit show, it'll be on us to make the call about bringing others in."

"All right. I'll need a background on Topher and

his half-sister, Piper. If shit gets dicey, the first place to start is close to home."

"Don't I know it? I'll get in contact with CCS. Now that they're operating at ninety percent, it won't take long. Check in after you meet the woman. I've got a feeling about this one."

"Yeah, it isn't like Topher. He's a by-the-numbers type of guy. To leave without telling someone, well, that's strange." Bear finally got through the red light and accelerated to keep up with the flow of traffic. "I'll call as soon as I know anything." He was concerned for his friend, not worried. Not yet. He wouldn't cross that bridge yet. But he could see the damn thing, and it looked like a big mother.

"Copy. I'm out."

Bear disconnected and followed the GPS prompts to an apartment complex outside the LSU campus. He parked and made his way to Topher's apartment. As a contract employee of Guardian, he maintained his badge to use when he was called up to work with the company. His gym was his life now. His brother was set, and Bear had fallen into owning and operating his gyms as naturally as a cat took after chasing mice. So, here he was, heading to Topher's apartment because his half-sister was sure something was wrong. He didn't have any weapons, not that he needed any, but when working for Guardian, he was normally strapped. He'd get with Sage to obtain a weapon if he needed one. God, he hoped like hell he didn't need one.

He knocked on the door and waited, then saw someone come to the peephole and look out. "I'm Bear McGowen." The door opened a crack, and he looked down at the woman he assumed was Piper. "Piper? May I come in?"

The woman blinked and nodded before slamming the door shut. He heard her remove the small chain that wouldn't have kept a pissed-off kitten out of the house, and then she opened the door again. Yeah, she was Topher's sister. She was slight, like Topher, with a runner's body. Her hair was the same color as her brother's, and she had the same nervous mannerisms. "Thank you for coming." She shut the door and walked into the apartment. "I've looked and looked. I can't find anything that indicates where he is or where he would have gone."

Bear noticed the apartment. It was just as he'd expect Topher's home to look. Everything was spotlessly clean and in its place. Squared away just like its owner. "Let's sit down and talk for a minute, okay?"

"Yeah, okay." The woman sat on one of the small couches and bounced back up. "Do you want something to drink?"

Bear sat down and shook his head. "No, thank you. So, once again, I'd like you to take me through how you came to call me."

The woman pulled her ponytail over her shoulder and spun a finger in the strands. "I left for a sabbatical. I was gone for three months. We regularly talked until the end of my time away."

"Sabbatical?" Bear heard the term in conjunction with the ministry, but she was a physicist.

"I went to Caltech to work with one of their physicists making strides in quantum computations based on loop theory. That hypothesis is the basis of my doctoral thesis. Christopher is not only my brother but my mentor, and he found the opportunity for me. Two weeks before I left Caltech, he told me he was going to check into some findings he'd recently uncovered. He promised me he'd be here when I got back." Piper popped up and walked to the window and back.

"What findings?"

The woman shook her head. "I'm not sure. He

has a project he's working on that he hasn't shared with me. He's been working on it for years. He said I didn't need to be involved with it and that it was for the government." She paced back to the window. "I can't find him. He isn't answering his phone. It isn't like him. He's not flighty."

"That I agree with. Have you searched this place?"

Piper stopped and jerked around. "Searched? For what?"

"For any indication of a struggle—"

"You think he's been kidnapped?" Piper's voice shot up so high that the dogs in the neighborhood should have started to howl.

"No, I didn't say that." Bear leaned forward. "Was anything out of place?"

"Ah … his closet door was open." Piper looked toward the hallway.

"Well, then, we can start there." As Bear stood up, Piper backed away. He got it. He was big and muscled, and Piper was slight and short in stature, maybe five feet two or three inches, so about a foot shorter than he was. "Would you show me his room, please?" Bear took in the rest of the apartment. The kitchen was immaculate, with no dishes in the sink or on the counter. The coffee pot was off and clean. "Do you stay here with Topher?"

Piper shook her head as she walked in front of him. "Not any longer. I did when I first came down." She passed a bedroom on the left. "That was my room."

Bear looked in. A tiny room with a single bed, a small dresser, and a closet. No pictures on the wall, no adornments of any kind. They walked farther down the hall to another doorway. "Here's Christopher's room." Piper turned on the light, and Bear gazed around the room. One picture was framed and hanging on the wall. A young Christopher and a middle-aged woman, probably his mother. On his dresser was a photo of Piper and him, both wearing race numbers and racing gear.

"You run marathons?"

Piper frowned at him. "How?" Bear pointed at the picture, and she smiled. "Oh, yes. It was something we had in common. We run to clear our minds. He got me into marathons." She stood in the middle of the room with her arms crossed. "The closet door was open. I shut it."

Bear nodded and headed to the closet, where he flipped a light switch on the wall outside the closet door, illuminating the contents.

Christopher's clothes hung at perfectly measured distances. Four hangers on the right-hand side were empty. His shoes were lined up on a shoe rack. Two spaces were empty. Bear looked at the top shelf. A space was clear—enough room for a small suitcase. The little things were starting to mound into more than concern, but he held back his rush to judge and did his job.

He moved into the bathroom—no toothbrush in the holder. Bear lifted the lid on the hamper. No dirty clothes. "Laundry room?"

Piper looked at him like he was crazy, but she led him to the double-door closet in the hall. He opened the doors and looked inside the washer and dryer. Empty. "He took a suitcase. His toothbrush is gone. How many suits did he have?" Bear asked as he went back to the bedroom.

"Three, one black, one blue, and one gray." Piper peered around him. "The gray suit is missing."

"And a pair of dress shoes."

"And his favorite running shoes." She moved to the dresser and opened a drawer. "He took running clothes." She shuffled through all the drawers. "Jeans, shirts."

"So, he went somewhere. The question is where. Have you looked through his office?"

"I did. It isn't as organized as his apartment." Piper ran her hand down her ponytail and started twirling a lock of hair. "The university office is about two miles away."

"Let's go," Bear said after taking one more look around the room.

Piper spoke when they made it to the sidewalk. "We can walk quicker than driving right now. There's a lacrosse game tonight."

"All right." Bear pulled out his phone and texted Sage as they walked.

Travel for Whitehead? Suitcase and clothes missing. Heading to office.

SAGE HIT him back almost immediately.

Requesting now.

Bear pocketed his phone. "Why hasn't the school reported him as missing?"

"He has a doctoral student teaching his classes. It isn't unusual for him not to be in the classroom for months at a time. He spends most of his time in the labs."

"And no one from the lab reported him missing?" Someone had to have noticed the guy wasn't around.

"I would have if I were here." Piper shook her head. "I shouldn't have left."

Bear glanced down at the woman. She was a nervous little bird, wasn't she? And she was worried. He'd stepped on that bridge, too. Damn it, what was going on? Topher was squared away. It wasn't like him to leave without a trace. The woman sighed again and mumbled something about never leaving again. He tried to reassure her. "What has happened is done. Guilt over what you should have have done is misplaced."

"But if I'd been here, I would've known he was gone."

"According to what you've said, he wouldn't have told you where he was going, right?"

She sighed and nodded. They crossed a street and headed across a vast area of green grass, heading to what looked like brick buildings clumped together. She stopped. "Wait. The government. They'd know where he was if you contacted them, right?"

"Do you know what branch he was working for?" The US government was a massive, sprawling monster with untold tentacles—those that could be seen and those that were invisible.

She deflated and turned to continue walking. "No."

"So, he didn't know you existed?" Bear asked to keep the conversation going. She might not talk as freely as he needed her to if she didn't trust him. That and he didn't want to scare her into a heart attack. She seemed wound tight. Not that he could blame her. *Where the hell are you Topher?*

"No. We met at a conference. It was the weirdest thing. One of my colleagues said, hey, you should talk to this guy. His last name is Whitehead, too." Piper snorted. "Whitehead isn't that rare of a name, but it was something to do while we were forced to socialize." She used her fingers to make quotations in the air. "I have severe social anxiety." She glanced up at him. "You scare me to death."

Bear laughed. "Obviously not. You're walking and talking."

Piper blinked and then smiled. "You're big."

"That I am. I'm also a friend of Topher's." He'd keep that point up in front of the conversation.

"Did he let you call him that?" She pointed in the direction they needed to go, and Bear pivoted with her.

"I never asked. I just shortened his name." Bear shrugged. Topher never said anything about it.

"Huh."

"Why?"

"He makes everyone call him Christopher. Chris isn't even an option. I think Topher would be a hard no for him, too." Piper pointed to a building and took a set of keys out of her pocket with an attached badge.

"Does that badge record each time you are in the building?"

"It does. It goes to security," Piper said as she slid her badge through the card reader, and the door opened.

"Can you get a copy of who came in? It could pin a closer date and time to when Topher left."

"They'll ask why." Piper jogged up the stairs, and Bear followed her.

"Fabricate a reason if you have to." Bear marched down a long hallway with Piper until she stopped at the door with Topher's name printed in gold.

She moved the key ring until she found the one she wanted and unlocked the door. Then, reaching in, she turned on the light. "Holy hell," Bear murmured, looking at the disaster that someone had decided was an office.

"He knows where everything is." Piper defended her brother.

"God, I hope so." Stacks of books and papers were piled around the office. A narrow trail led to the back of the desk. Bear picked up a pad of paper and squinted. "What in the world is this chicken scratch? A foreign language?"

"What?" Piper stood on her tiptoes to look at what he was holding, then dropped down. "Oh, that's his shorthand."

"It's indecipherable." Bear turned the page and shook his head.

"No, I can read it. But that's after years of working with him." Piper pointed. "Those are essays he thought were brilliant and kept with the student's permission. Over here are the course syllabuses. These are his notebooks on lab experiments dating back to when he started here at the college. Over here are notes from department meetings. This is correspondence with the college and with associates in the field."

Bear's eyes bounced from stack to stack as she pointed at them. "A date book or calendar?"

"On his computer." She motioned to the laptop on the desk.

"He didn't take his laptop?"

"Not that one. That's just for school. His computer is decked out." She opened the top drawer with her keys. "And gone."

"All right. Let's look at his calendar." Piper opened the laptop and typed in the password. "Did he share that with you? The password?"

She chuffed. "Yeah, it's 'password.'"

"You're shitting me?"

"That's vulgar, and I assure you, I'm not." She sighed. "He didn't care who saw his schedule or what he had on this computer. Here's his calendar." She waved at the laptop and stepped to the side.

"I'm sorry, it was vulgar," Bear acknowledged as he stared at the screen. "It looks like it's all recurring appointments." Bear looked at office hours, lab time, and meetings with university department heads. "How could anyone not have missed him?" Topher had meetings at least three times a week. Nobody but Piper looked for him. That was … sad.

Damn, his gut was tightening, and he didn't like the reason for it. He could see now why Piper was worked up.

"Because he doesn't always go to these meetings. He's tenured, and his work brings the university money. A lot of money, Mr. McGowen. Millions."

Bear stood up straight and looked down at her. "How?"

"Donations. Since he started working here, the physics department has doubled in size and capacity. Scholars from around the world flock here to work with him. He's a genius. But he hates the teaching aspect of the job. That's why no one missed him in the classroom or for office hours."

"There has to be something."

"It would take a month to go through everything here." Piper sighed. "Am I being stupid?"

Bear shook his head. She definitely wasn't being stupid. Something was off. He couldn't put his finger on it, but the absence was not like Topher. "No. I don't think so. Cautious, yes. Topher is lucky to have you in his life."

She shook her head. "I'm the lucky one. He understands me."

Bear felt his phone vibrate and glanced down at the message. "Have you checked Topher's house?"

Piper jerked her head back. "He doesn't have a house."

His eyebrows rose at that comment. A secret from Piper? Maybe they weren't as close as Piper thought. "According to this, he does. Care to take a ride with me?" He pocketed the phone and stared at the deer-in-the-headlights look he was getting from the woman in front of him. "Or you could meet me at the address and call someone you know to tell them where you'll be and with whom."

Piper swallowed hard and blinked owlishly. "I'll go with you."

Bear could see the fear in her eyes, but the woman battled through it. "Then let's go. My car is parked in front of Topher's apartment."

Bear threw a quick text to his managers and let them know he'd been recalled by the military for a mission. That was the cover story he used when he worked for Guardian. No one ever questioned it, and everyone thought he was in the reserves. They knew the drill. They were in charge, and he trusted them completely. With work covered, he could work on finding Topher without distractions.

CHAPTER 2

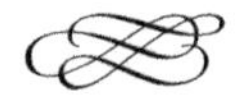

Piper buckled her seatbelt and prayed she wasn't getting into a car with a serial killer. Bear McGowen was massive. *Massive.* His arms were covered in tattoos, and when he bent them, his biceps were bigger than her waist. She was insane for getting into a car with him. The man was a complete stranger, and she had no idea if he was a decent person. Okay, yes, Christopher trusted him, but Bear could be completely untethered from reality. Her brother had said it'd been years since he'd worked with the guy. She swallowed hard. Why hadn't she taken her meds? Why did she say she'd ride with him? With a sigh, she rubbed her forehead. Stranger danger. Her hands were trembling.

She should have called the police. But Christopher didn't want that. He trusted Bear. Yet, the man could snap her in half like a dry twig. That mind picture didn't help. She was in the rental vehicle with him. She could do it. Maybe. Should she get out? Probably. But if he could find her brother, it would be worth the ulcer and the nervous breakdown that was bound to result from driving away from campus with a stranger. Dear Lord, how did she get into such a mess?

As her hands moved from trembling to outright shaking, she sat on them and watched him plug in an address to the GPS. "That's the old side of town."

"Surprising he didn't tell you about his house."

"Not really. He's a private person." But she was hurt he hadn't shared the fact he owned a house. "Maybe he rents it out." That would be like him. Renting it to a student for next to nothing.

"Could be. We'll find out when we get there."

As Bear drove out of the parking lot and into traffic, Piper pulled out her phone and dialed campus security. "Hi, Phil, it's Piper from the Physics department. Could you email me the sign-in sheet for the last month?"

"Sure, I'm going to need a reason," the paid security guard answered.

"A rash of forgetting to lock up. Nothing was stolen or missing. We need to remind a few people to be more security conscious."

"Okay. I'll send it to you as soon as the boss signs off on it."

"Thank you." She blew out a breath after she hung up. "I detest liars."

"It was a white lie, and it could help us find Topher," Bear said as he turned at a light.

"I still don't like it." Piper crossed her arms.

"Been burned by lies?" Bear asked.

Piper snorted, "Ha, my father kept my brother from me for my entire life. My mom didn't even know he'd been married before. She forgave him. I'm still working on it."

"It takes all kinds to make the world go around," Bear murmured.

"I'm unsure if you're talking about my father or me." She couldn't read the man. She wasn't the best in social settings, and her anxiety was ratcheting up being in a car with a man she didn't know. Granted, she'd called him into it, and as she kept reminding herself, Christopher trusted him. Honestly, that was the only reason she'd opened the door. It was the only reason she was in a vehicle heading to a house she didn't know Christopher owned.

"I was speaking of your father. Although I don't know his rationale for not speaking of his past, it does seem strange." Bear put on his blinker and waited for an oncoming car to pass before he turned.

She agreed with Bear's logic. Bear. She blurted out, "Is Bear your real name?"

He chuckled. "It is. My dad wanted to name me Grizzly, but my mom reached a happy medium with him. My brother is Wolf. Are you named after a plane?"

Piper cocked her head. "No, I was named after my great-aunt on my mother's side. Why?"

The guy looked at her like she had three heads. "You've never heard of a Piper Cub? The airplane?"

"No." She lifted her phone and hit up the search engine. Her hands were still shaking, but not as much. "Oh, wow. No, I had no idea." She scrolled and read about the little aircraft. "Why did your parents name you after animals?" she asked as she scrolled.

"My mom and dad were hippies from a bygone

era. They liked the names and felt that we'd grow up strong. They weren't wrong."

"Is your brother as big as you?"

Bear shrugged. "As tall, but not as much bulk. He's a neurosurgeon—or soon will be. He finishes his residency next month."

Piper nodded. "I thought about medicine, but I don't do well with people."

"You're doing okay with me." Bear looked over and smiled at her.

Piper shook her head. "Outside, maybe. Internally, not so much." She was one quick move from losing it. "Christopher liked you. He trusted you. That's the only reason I'm not freaking out." However, her foot was constantly tapping on the floorboard of the car.

"How did you go to Caltech if you have social anxiety?"

"Medication." She sighed. "I'm not ashamed of having to use it. But I only take them when I'm extremely stressed." As unashamed as she wanted to be, she still felt the need to defend herself.

"I wouldn't suspect you would be. If it helps you do what you want, then I say it's a good thing." He didn't look at her as he spoke and decelerated. "This is the street."

Piper found an address. “This side is even, so it's on your side.” She glanced at the number again. “Three blocks down.”

Bear sped up a little but didn’t surpass the posted speed limit. Thankfully. If the man was a bad driver, she might have jumped out of the vehicle because she was wound that tight. She hated not being on schedule and not having a routine. The unpredictable events during her day upset her to the point of a complete meltdown. That was why academia was a perfect place for her. Routine and schedules, day in and day out. She could become lost in the drone of teaching and find a sense of peace with life. It was something she’d rarely had until Christopher convinced her to move south to be with him. He was her routine, and even though *he* wasn’t consistent, *she* was consistent in her interaction with him. He was her anchor in the choppy waters of people and expectations.

The neighborhood was nice. Cozy homes dotted an old, tree-lined street. Children rode bicycles and scooters down the sidewalk.

“Here.” Bear pulled into the driveway of a small ranch-style home. The porch on the front was shaded on either side by ivy trellises.

There were no cars that Piper could see, and no one came outside. "Maybe no one is home."

"Let's go see."

"You mean go to the door?" Piper pointed to the house. "We don't know them."

"How do we know if it's rented or people are living here?" Bear opened his door.

"Because the lawn is mowed, and ..." Bear shut his door and walked in front of the SUV.

Nope. She wouldn't do it. She wouldn't go to that door. She watched as he walked up the steps to the porch that ran the length of the house and knocked on the door. Piper shrunk down. Her shoulders were almost to her ears. She slid down even farther when Bear cupped his hands and looked into the window by the door. He returned to the door, looked up and down the street, and took something out of his pocket. He worked the handle, and then ... *He walked in!*

No, no, no. He did not just break into that house. Dear Lord, she needed to call the police. But would she be an accessory? Yes, damn it.

After waiting several minutes in a near panic, she watched as Bear came out of the house and toward the vehicle, opening her door. "It's Christopher's house. He's been doing work here."

"How do you know?" Right. He was probably spreading plastic sheets on the floor so he could kill her without making a mess. Stupid. She was stupid. She was going to die. Christopher would never be found.

Bear smiled at her. "I promise I'm not an ax murderer. Come see."

She narrowed her gaze at him. "That's what an ax murderer would say, isn't it?"

Bear seemed to think about that for a minute. "Probably."

"You broke into the house, didn't you? We'll get arrested."

"No, I promise you we won't." Bear opened the door wider.

Piper shook her head. "I can't." Nope. If he wasn't an ax murderer, he could be the Boston Strangler reincarnated. Or the Unabomber. *Stop! Lord, this is not helping find Christopher.*

"Piper, I need your help. There's a huge room full of his writing. I need to know what he was working on."

"For the government? Isn't that breaching some protocol?" She so didn't want to get in any trouble. Her eyes bulged at that thought. She was neck-deep in a breaking-and-entering scenario.

"I work for the government, Piper. I work for Guardian Security. That's why your brother told you to call me. We will not be arrested. I need you to come read this stuff for me."

Right, like Christopher wouldn't have told her that? "How do I know that's true?" She was shaking so badly that her teeth were clattering.

Bear took out his wallet and crouched down to look at her at eye level. "This is my badge, and these are my credentials." He handed the wallet to her, and she stared at the silver badge and then looked at the holographic embossed credentials. They looked official, but she wouldn't know. She'd never seen either a badge or ID like that up close.

"Please? We need to figure out what happened to Christopher." Bear extended his hand. Damn it, he pulled the only trump card that would win the debate. Piper took his hand and started to get out of the car, but the seatbelt strangled her. She reached back and released the belt.

Bear took her hand and shut the door as soon as she got out. He didn't push her, letting her walk up to the door at her own pace. Thank goodness for that, or she would have rolled into a ball and succumbed to a panic attack. She looked inside before stepping foot into the house. It was small, with old furniture. There were pictures on the wall. Pictures of Christopher and his mother. She stepped in and went straight to the wall. Pictures of Christopher with trophies. Track, science club, soccer. She smiled at the happiness she saw on his face. "This must be his mom's house."

"I think so. Come look at this." He walked through the living room and down the hallway, stopping at an open doorway. Piper moved beside him and blinked. Pictures and documents lined the walls. Strings of red thread went from one to the next. Blue thread combined other articles and one document that had been redacted. She walked in, taking in the magnitude of the work the room displayed. She moved to one of the many redacted documents. "*This* is the game."

"What game?"

Piper jumped at Bear's voice. He moved silently for such a big man. "We figured out an algorithm to determine how many letters or words could be in a blacked-out box based on the document's font. Christopher said he was thinking about building a game." She touched the word written in shorthand above the redacted portion of the report. "He figured out what information was deleted."

"This is his shorthand again, isn't it."

"It is." She turned to look at Bear. "But what does all of this mean?"

"That's what we're going to find out." Bear rubbed his neck. "I'm going to order some food. We could be here all night."

She nodded, barely hearing what he'd said. Bear wasn't an ax murderer, and no plastic sheets were waiting for her demise. What she found in the room, though, was instantly enthralling. The ingenuity of her brother was off the charts. Where would Christopher start? Where was his solve for X in the equation of the documents, pictures, articles, and notes?

She walked the walls, looking for an origination point. She could hear Bear talking in the other portion of the house, but his presence was insignificant. She stopped in front of a denial of a report that Christopher had requested through the Freedom of Information Act. She tapped the document and stared at it. *Here. This article.* This could be the solution for X portion of the problem. The blue, red, and yellow strings all segued in some fashion to that point. There was where she would start. She glanced around and saw three journals. The first was filled with notes and dated. The second, dated even earlier, and the third ... The third had pages torn out, leaving most of the journal intact and blank. Piper picked up a mechanical pencil from alongside the journals. It was time to figure out where Christopher was and what he was doing.

CHAPTER 3

Bear dialed Sage and waited for his friend and boss to pick up. "What's up?"

"The house is a gold mine. Topher has been doing some research." Bear looked back at the room and watched Piper's hand move from document to article to picture as she moved along the wall.

"On what?"

"I have no idea, but his sister is here, and she can read his shorthand. The man was searching for something, that's for sure."

"Something that would put him in jeopardy?"

"Maybe. Did we get anything on any travel that Topher may have booked?"

"Not yet. We're in the queue, and it should be coming at any time. I'm going to come over. I'll be there in about two and a half hours."

Bear frowned, perplexed. "Why?"

"The more eyes on that information, the better. We can work in shifts, so one of us is fresh. The bosses are keenly interested in what's going on. Christopher's phone is going to voicemail, so it's either turned off or out of juice."

"This isn't sounding good." Bear walked out and stood on the porch looking across the street at the middle-class homes. "I'm going to get back inside and try to find a starting point with all those documents. His sister will be the key to a lot of this. She's the only one who can read that mess she calls shorthand."

"I'll be there soon. Do you need anything?"

"A computer. One that we can access Guardian on. My gut is telling me that something bad has happened, and the reason for it is in the documents and articles lining the walls of that room. I also need a weapon. I flew down and wasn't active, so I didn't bring one."

"You got it. Get to work. I'll be there soon."

Bear disconnected and pulled up his delivery

app. He plugged in the address and ordered food and drinks before returning to the room.

Piper was sitting on the floor cross-legged, staring at the wall in front of her. She had a notebook and a pencil and was moving her finger over an article printed on bond paper. "Did you find something?" Bear asked.

She jumped, and the pencil went flying. "Oh, crud!"

"Sorry, I didn't mean to startle you." Bear bent down, picked up the pencil, and returned it to her.

"No, I get tunnel vision when I'm working. But look at this. I think I found the starting point for his work. This is an article from a Newspaper in Venezuela." She pointed to a yellowing piece of paper on the wall.

Bear sat down beside her and leaned forward to translate the article from Spanish to English. Piper picked up her phone. "I think it says there was a government raid on a building. The building was then placed on quarantine due to radioactive materials."

Bear shook his head. "Not quite. It was an abandoned warehouse, and it was restricted by the government, who warned people to stay out due to the possibility of radioactive residue." He glanced at the date. "Three days after we left Cuba."

"You read Spanish?" Piper sighed when he nodded. "Good, there are a lot of articles here, and I had to type that into the translation app." She turned to him. "Does this have something to do with why you were in Cuba?"

Bear lifted an eyebrow. "I can't discuss that. Classified."

Piper pointed to herself. "I have a Top Secret Clearance."

"Ah, but you don't need to know at this point, and my organization would have to confirm your clearance before I could talk to you about it."

"Well, that's going to make this awkward, right?" She waved at the wall. "We should be able to work together."

"You're right." Bear took his phone out of his back pocket and dialed Sage.

"What's up?" He could tell Sage was driving.

"Can we get clearance for Piper Whitehead to be read into our Cuba mission and anything else we might discuss? She says she has a TS clearance."

"She doesn't just say it. She does," Piper mumbled beside him.

Sage chuckled. "I'll make the call. We should be able to confirm and get approval ASAP."

"Thanks. See you in a few." Bear hung up.

"Your boss is coming here?"

"He lives nearby. The more eyes on the information, the better."

"Different perspectives, yes, that makes sense." She tapped her notebook with her pencil. "This is the oldest article I've found. All his linear processes are aligned through this article, so while it's not where *he* started, it's where the problem starts. This is what he was trying to solve."

"A warehouse in Venezuela?" Bear stared at the lines wrapped around push pins.

"No." She shook her head. "What was in the warehouse."

She stared at the wall, and Bear stared at her. "What do you mean?"

"Christopher's biggest fear was nuclear proliferation. He worked with the Nuclear Regulatory Commission on the accountability of radioactive material. The US is good about keeping track of those materials. Russia? When the wall fell, a lot of people made a fortune selling bits and pieces of uranium. Christopher wouldn't talk about what he knew from his work with the government." Piper glanced at him.

"He said it was classified over my clearance." She shrugged and stared at the wall, her eyes moving from the original article to the one on the right and above it. "He thinks there's enriched uranium out there." She leaned back and stared up toward the ceiling at the reports at the top of the wall. "Pages are missing from this notebook. I think he found it."

"Can you follow his logic and find out what he knew?" Bear could translate the articles from Spanish for her and keep track of the information once the computer arrived.

"He makes intuitive leaps." Piper put her finger on the original article and followed the yellow thread. She lifted to her knees and walked on them to the next report. "This is a Freedom of Information Act request asking for documents from the Nuclear Regulatory Commission on known violations of United States laws governing the transportation of nuclear materials."

"Did he get a response?"

She shook her head. "It was denied. But he circled the office that denied the request. I don't know why. Then he wrote E1 on the side."

Bear moved over beside her. "Odd. Why would that be circled?"

Piper nodded. "It's in red ink." She tapped the circle. "He thought it was important." She leaned back and grabbed the notebook, and Bear watched as she wrote down the information. Shaking her head, she looked at the request. "It could take months to figure out what he found."

"What if we fed the information into a computer?" Bear was grasping at straws, but his gut told him they didn't have months.

She blinked and looked at him. "I don't have the talent to devise a program like that."

Bear nodded. "My company does." He picked up his phone again.

"You are a needy person." Sage chuckled when he answered.

"We need a programmer. The information is so vast it could take months to sort through it and find the connections that Topher found."

"Can it be done virtually?" Sage asked, and Bear repeated the question to Piper.

She nodded. "We can feed the information on each document to them. If we keep it linear, as he has it sorted, we should be able to find what connected these documents."

"Yes," Bear told Sage.

"I'll call it in. I'm not sure where we'll fall in the priority stack," Sage acknowledged.

"Thanks." Bear discontinued the call.

Piper jumped and gasped when there was a knock on the door. "The police?" she hissed.

"No, our food." Bear chuckled and stood up. "Come on. We need to eat in order to work through the night." He extended his hand to her.

Piper looked at his hand and then at him before accepting his offer of assistance. He honestly believed Piper thought he was some sort of deranged killer. But she'd stopped shaking like a leaf, so maybe she'd made up her mind that he wouldn't order Chianti and have some fava beans for dinner.

Bear let go of her hand as soon as she stood and headed to the front door. Piper was washing her hands in the sink when he returned to the kitchen. He opened the bag and pulled the food out.

"Oh, thank goodness." Piper looked at the salads he'd ordered. "I don't eat junk." She smiled at him.

That was the first time he'd seen that expression. She was a beautiful woman. Bear lowered his eyes and mentally shook his head. He wasn't there to notice things like that. He was there to find his friend. Topher's sister was not included in that mission. "I figured." She ran marathons, and when he could be, Topher was very particular about what he ate when they were on the mission together. Bear didn't eat junk either, but he did eat, and the snacks on the airplane weren't enough to keep a mouse alive.

He pulled out two containers, one with chicken and the other with steak. "Protein for the salads."

After she selected the chicken, he took the steak. She looked at him once and then again. He chuckled. "Do you have a question?"

"You don't eat like this all the time, do you? I mean, you're big." She took a bite of her spinach salad.

"Actually, I have to eat a lot more than an average person would. I lift weights and train six days a week, so I burn a lot of calories and carbs. My diet is regimented. I stick to it because I feel better when I do."

She nodded. "I get that. If I eat junk, I can feel it when I run. What do you train for?"

Bear didn't mind the questions. At least she'd calmed down a bit. At one point on the drive over, he thought her foot would tap a hole through the floorboard. He knew he could be intimidating, but he didn't want to scare Topher's sister.

"I study martial arts."

"What kind?" She stabbed some more spinach and veggies.

"Muay Thai and Jiu-Jitsu and a newer discipline called Goju-Ryu." He rarely talked about his expertise in any of the arts he studied. Piper didn't need to know that he could kill a person with his hands.

"And you work for Guardian?"

"Part-time," he answered. "I own several gyms that specialize in proper movement and technique when lifting. We offer classes in Jiu-Jitsu for little ones. After they reach the age to go into school, they can transfer to a regular dojo."

Piper blinked at him. "Why would you want to teach babies how to fight?"

Bear smiled even though he cringed inside. The question was asked far too often. "We aren't teaching them how to fight. We teach proper movements, patterns, the mind and body connection, discipline, and respect. If children are taught to respect tradition and listen to their teachers at a young age, they'll have a foot up when they start school. Three, four, and five year old's do not need to know how to fight. They need people who are there for them, who will teach them, and listen to them."

Piper sat down her fork and stared at him for a moment. "That sounded like you've said it a few times."

"When I started the program for disadvantaged youth, it was met with resistance. Mind you, not by the community I was serving, but by some people who saw what I was doing. I use my money to buy the children's uniforms with knee pads. As they grow out of the uniform, I have them cleaned and inspected and then give them to another child who can use them. I have a backroom full of uniforms." He chuckled and shook his head. I teach all the classes free of charge. We focus on respect, tradition, and repetition of movement in the correct form."

"You like kids?" Piper leaned her chin on her hand and stared at him.

Bear shrugged. "I do. They're a hell of a lot easier to work with than adults."

Piper laughed. The sound was almost musical. "I prefer adults. I don't know how to talk to children."

"Like you would anyone else." Bear ate another bite of food. "You just have to be kind."

Piper lowered her eyes. "I've been told I'm too abrupt."

"Abrupt?" He glanced over at her. "Who told you that?"

She shrugged. "It doesn't matter. I am abrupt to a degree. I usually say whatever is on my mind."

"That isn't a bad thing." Bear preferred that mode of conversation. Pretense and hiding behind lies royally chapped his ass.

"I don't think so, but some do." She cut some chicken with her plastic spork and knife. "How much trouble do you think Christopher is in?"

Bear put down his utensils and leaned back in the chair. He waited until she lifted her eyes to look at him. "I'm not sure. My gut is telling me he fell into something."

"Are you worried?" Piper's eyes misted a bit.

He nodded. "I am, but I'm a bit overprotective of Topher. It was my job to make sure he made it through the mission we were on."

Piper's eyes widened to the size of silver dollars. Long lashes framed the dark brown of her eyes. Bear blinked when he realized he was staring at Topher's sister and shouldn't be thinking about the things that danced through his mind. But, damn, the woman was attractive.

"Was it dangerous? The mission? Christopher didn't talk much about it, but he did talk about you and the others. He said you were the best at what you do."

"I'm sure he was exaggerating, but the mission had its moments." Sage was shot, then the run to the gate at Guantanamo Bay, working with black-market operatives and traveling through Cuba with the niece of a notorious criminal, all while hiding from a corrupt communist regime. Yeah, that time with Creed and the crew had its moments.

"Christopher said you were probably the bravest man he'd ever met." Piper took a bite of her salad.

"Ha, well, I'm not any braver than the next man. When a mission fits my talent, I'm called up for it. I get the job done." He agreed to put his life on the line for the betterment of the whole—in the military and now with Guardian. It was a risk he didn't hesitate to take.

"Thank you for dinner, by the way." Piper nodded to his empty salad bowl and her half-eaten salad. "I'll save the rest of mine unless you'd like it?"

Bear shook his head. "I'm good, thank you." She ate like a bird and was as skittish as one, too, although she wasn't acting afraid of him now.

She put the plastic cap back on the salad. "I'd like to take another look at those documents on the first wall. Maybe he sorted them by relevance." Piper headed to the refrigerator as he stood—that same moment, a crash of glass and the report of a weapon sounded.

Bear lunged toward Piper and tackled her, rolling them to the far corner of the kitchen. Her scream was muffled as he held her to his chest. Another crash of glass, that time from the bedroom. *Fuck!* "Stay here! Don't move!"

He low-crawled to the hallway and then sprinted to the bedroom. Flames spread from the floor to the walls. Bear darted in, grabbed the notebooks, and tore documents and articles from the wall.

Piper was beside him, pulling documents down. "Call the fire department!" Bear roared at her.

She ignored him and yelled, "These documents are too important!"

Bear agreed with her, but the people next door didn't need to perish because of them, and the way the fire was spreading…

Bear turned Piper, put the notebooks in her hand, and gave her his phone on top of all the papers he'd pulled from the wall. "Fire Department, now!" He shoved her down the hallway before turning and grabbing as much off the walls as possible. Documents ripped in half as he grabbed at them. He moved from report to report and pulled down the articles he could see. Black smoke tumbled from the ceiling.

"Bear! You have to come out!"

Bear's arms were filled with papers as he looked back to reprimand Piper for coming back into the room, but she wasn't there. Flames had blocked him from the hallway and the window across the room. The hallway was the shortest distance. "Stand back!" he roared and gaged the fire he'd need to run through. *Damn it, damn it, damn it!* He ripped off his shirt and shoved all the papers into it. Holding it to his chest Bear launched through the flames. He hit the wall across from the room, and Piper was on him with a wet towel.

"Your arm is on fire!"

Bear dropped the documents, and Piper's towel covered his forearm. The hair on his arm had singed. "Papers." He pointed to the bundle and coughed.

"We have to get out!" Piper grabbed the bundle and then his hand. They sprinted out of the house into a mist of water. Several neighbors were spraying water from their hoses onto the house. Piper kept hold of his hand as a police car pulled up. "Papers in the truck." Bear bent down, trying to draw in air.

Piper nodded and headed that way. He watched as she put his shirt on top of the notebooks and the papers he'd shoved in her hand earlier. He dropped his head again and tried to stop coughing.

"Are you the owner?" Shiny black shoes appeared on the ground where he was staring. Bear reached into his back pocket and flipped open the case, still bending down, still trying to stop coughing. He knew the badge and ID were visible. The cop shifted. "This is Bravo twenty-three. We need an ambulance at my location."

Bear shook his head.

"Can it, buddy. You've been singed pretty good," The cop said. "At least let the EMTs take a look at you."

Bear was going to reply, but the wail of a fire truck's siren defeated that thought. He looked toward his truck. Piper was on her knees beside it. Bear staggered over to where she was and dropped onto his ass beside her.

"They shot at us." Piper shook her head and stared at the house. "What was Christopher doing?" She dropped to her butt beside him.

Bear put his arm around her and pulled her into him. Not because she needed the comfort but because he did. Fuck, that fire had spread fast. Too fast. Some kind of accelerant had to be used, and he didn't smell gasoline. Someone wanted the evidence gone.

Bear watched as the fire ripped through the roof of the old house. A huge arc of water blasted through the air from fire hoses. Bear watched as the firefighters worked, but nothing was registering, even though he saw everything. Because if they wanted the evidence gone, that meant that Topher had told them where it was. Bear dropped his chin to the top of Piper's head and closed his eyes. The chances of Topher being alive and well had just lowered to almost none.

CHAPTER 4

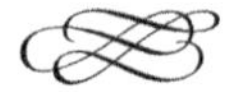

Piper sat beside the big man who'd risked his life to save Christopher's papers. The large arm around her was comforting as Christopher's childhood home burned. The EMTs had come and gone. Bear refused to be seen, and they couldn't persuade him to change his mind. Piper hadn't tried.

"Sir, we're going to need a statement."

Piper looked up and froze. A police officer was towering above them. Bear's arm tightened around her almost imperceivably. "I'm working with Guardian Security. We were shot at, and some accelerant was thrown into the bedroom window before it was set ablaze."

"And your name is Christopher Whitehead?" the police officer asked.

"No, your partner saw my credentials. I'm Bear McGowen. I'm investigating the disappearance of Christopher Whitehead. It's an ongoing investigation, and I can't say more about it." Bear coughed. She could feel his chest vibrate against her arm.

"And you, ma'am?" The officer turned his attention to her.

She answered honestly. "I'm Piper Whitehead. Christopher's sister. This is … was Christopher's house."

"I'm afraid you both need to come with us to the station. There are a lot of holes in this story."

"Where is my phone?" Bear asked her. She reached into the back pocket of her jeans and handed it to him. He didn't move his arm from around her as he made his call. "We were shot at, and the house was torched. We're fine. One of Baton Rouge's finest wants us to go into the station. Yep. Okay. Yeah, we'll be here." Bear dropped the phone on the driveway and looked up at the officer. "You'll be receiving a call soon."

The officer looked at him. "Bravo Twenty-three, I'm going to need a supervisor out here."

Bear grunted and turned back to look at the house. Piper followed his gaze. Billows of black smoke rolled upward to the night sky. "Bear?"

He turned to her. "Yeah?"

"He's not okay, is he?" Piper knew he wasn't. She'd had a bad feeling since the first time he didn't call her back. "I waited too long to call you, didn't I?"

He sighed and tightened his hold on her momentarily. "I have a feeling that even if you had called me from Caltech, tonight's events would have happened."

"Because he's not okay." She nodded, agreeing with herself. "Someone shot at us." She wrapped her arms around her middle and leaned forward. Her gut dropped, and she started to shiver. "They burned down his house. This isn't good. He's in trouble. He's not okay. You're going to help me find him, though, right?"

Bear sighed. "We'll work to find out what's going on. We'll work together, and we'll find him."

Piper dropped her head onto his shoulder, and he rested his chin on her head again. He didn't tell her she was stupid or to stop overreacting. She was right. Christopher was not okay. Cocooned by his big body, she let the tears she'd held back for far too long fall because she knew in her heart that they might not find him alive.

PIPER JERKED awake when a new voice sounded beside her. How in the hell had she fallen asleep?

Bear's hand ran up and down her back. She'd cried until she was exhausted ... God, she hadn't had a panic attack, had she? She tensed and thought back. No, she was just mentally exhausted. She'd fallen asleep.

"Are you all right? Is she?" She saw cowboy boots and jeans.

Bear's voice rumbled under her ear, "We're okay. It's been a hell of a night."

Piper snorted in agreement, then lifted her head and looked at the man crouched beside them.

"Hey, I'm Sage Browning. We work together." He pointed at Bear. "How about we get you guys out of here?"

"The police want us to go with them," Piper said and sat up. Bear's arm slipped off her, and she immediately missed its weight and warmth, which brought a slew of questions to mind. Why did she miss it? What made her feel so safe with a man she'd just met? Why was he different than every other person on the planet? It had to be the fire and guns. A traumatic response to what had happened. *Right?*

"They've been advised that isn't going to happen." Sage shook his head. "Is there a place we can go to talk?" Sage stood and offered her a hand.

Piper hesitated and glanced at Bear. He nodded, and she reached up and took Sage's hand. The man pulled her up and released her immediately.

"Come on, up you go." He clasped hands with Bear, braced himself, and pulled the man up. "Dude, where did you lose your shirt?"

"I didn't lose it." Bear motioned to the rental. "I needed something to keep Topher's research papers safe."

"When he ran through the fire. His arm is burned." Piper filled in what Bear didn't say.

Sage looked at her and then at Bear. "Since when did you become fireproof?"

"I'm fine. The hair on my arm is singed off, no blisters, no pain." He rolled his arm in proof.

"He's been coughing." Piper felt like she was tattling. Maybe she was.

Bear looked down at her, narrowed his eyes, and then winked at her. He turned back to Sage, and Piper tried to understand what that was about. Why would he wink at her? Maybe it was a tic? People got tics when they were mad. Her father did. Was he that mad at her?

"I think we should check on Topher's apartment." Bear stretched and winced.

Oh, God. No, Christopher's apartment? "Do you think they destroyed it, too?"

"I can find out." Sage walked away from them and up to the cop on the scene. The fire trucks were emptying the water from the hoses.

"There's nothing left of his mom's house," Piper solemnly noted, gazing at the charred remains.

Bear nodded. "Accelerant. It made the fire burn hot and fast. The age of the house did the rest."

"We can go to my apartment." Piper blurted out the invite. "It should be safe to talk there, right?"

Bear glanced at the house. "I'm not sure any place in Baton Rouge is safe right now."

Piper shivered and rubbed her arms. "They're sending a unit to the apartment complex," Sage said as he crossed the lawn.

"Send one to Piper's apartment, too." Bear

moved to the rental and started unloading the papers from his shirt.

Sage asked for her address, and she gave it to him. Then he went back to the officer. Piper waited until Bear had his shirt on before stacking the papers scattered all over the seat. "If the answer to who did this is in these papers, I will find it." She spoke to herself. It was a promise to Christopher. He'd never get the memories inside his house back, and she couldn't help him with that, but she could help figure out what had happened and where he'd gone.

Bear shrugged on his shirt. "Have you looked at the notebooks?"

"Only to see the dates. He's been working on this for a long time." She picked one up, cracked it open to a random page, and read, *"There is no way to prove involvement between the agencies I originally suspected. However, if we change the original supposition to just the players, there may be a connection."* She looked up at Bear. "He sounds like a conspiracy theorist here. But he wasn't. I know he wasn't."

"We have proof of that fact." Bear nodded to the blackened shell of a house.

Piper held the notebook to her chest and stared

at the structure. She knew the anatomy of a fire, of how the flame consumed oxygen and burned through combustibles, but Bear was right. Some kind of accelerant was used.

"The fire started in the bedroom."

Bear stopped stacking papers and looked down at her. "It did."

"So, someone else knew about his research. But how?" She couldn't put the dots together.

"A question we'll figure out sooner or later."

"There are too many questions." Piper put the notebook down beside the pile of papers. "We need answers."

Bear smiled at her. "And we'll get them. Together."

"Okay, Christopher and Piper's places have been broken into," Sage said as he came up to them. "We aren't going to stick around to see the damage. You're coming with me. If they follow us, it'll be evident, and we'll end it."

Piper's stomach dropped. She didn't have much, but … her clothes, pictures … *Could this night get any worse?* "Where are we going? I need clothes. What about calling the insurance company? I can't leave now." Piper turned away from the men and walked to the end of the driveway. The fire truck started up, startling her. She turned to her right. Headlights flicked on, and she was momentarily blinded. The car revved its engine and lurched toward her. Piper froze. She knew she had to move, but …

The jarring explosion of energy that hit her drove her off her feet. She closed her eyes and curled as she hit the pavement. She was rolled and then covered. The fast pop, pop, pop of gunfire exploded around her. Piper pushed on Bear. He rolled off her, and his grip put her on top of him. "Are you okay?"

Bear held her to his chest. "I'm okay. Are you?" He loosened his grip on her.

"What? Who?" She lifted onto her elbows on top of Bear.

The car had skipped the sidewalk and drove through the yard. She could see the tracks. Sage jogged over. "The bastard got away, but the unit that was here is on his car's ass."

Piper hissed as he helped her up and glanced down at Bear. "Your arm!"

He lifted it and looked at the raw scrape where the asphalt had torn away his skin. "I'll be fine."

Sage once again offered Bear a hand. "This is getting to be a routine, my man."

Bear groaned, "Yeah, let's not continue it."

"Check your vehicle for trackers. I'll get with the bosses. BRPD needs to keep us in the loop." Sage trotted over to the fire truck and waved them on as he put the phone up to his ear.

Piper watched him direct the fire truck off the curb and step out of the way as it rumbled by. She was in trouble. The stress of … everything … was too much. She walked up to Bear, put a trembling hand on his chest, and looked up at him. "I don't like this. I'm afraid. I want my brother home, and I want to go back to my routine. I don't like it when my routines are messed with." She shook her head. The motion became faster and faster. Tears came to her eyes again. She lowered her voice. "I can't. I'm so scared. Please, please don't make me do this. I need to be safe. I need my medicine. Oh, God, please. Bear, I need Christopher. He knows what to do. I'm going to …" Piper started to cry.

Strong arms wrapped around her. "I've got you. I won't let anything happen to you."

Piper gasped. She could feel the fear choking her. She had no control. Her lips started tingling, and she knew she was in danger and wasn't safe.

She heard him talking, and then he picked her up. She hung onto him because he was the only thread of sanity she could cling to. The panic attack consumed her. It consumed everything. Her mind swirled, and she started hyperventilating. She knew what was next. She could hear Bear's voice as she entered the black tunnel.

CHAPTER 5

Sage jogged over to him. "Is she okay? What the hell happened? She was up and moving. Did she hit her head when you tackled her?"

Bear could see the terror in the woman's eyes before she passed out. The way she gripped his shirt and begged him to help her. He'd never felt more helpless in his life. "No, I don't think so. I think she had a panic attack. She said she gets them." Bear held the limp woman in his arms. "She was hyperventilating. Man, I'm telling you this shit is getting deep and quick." Bear carried her to the rental and carefully put her in the passenger seat, using the power remote to lean the seat back.

"It would've been a hell of a lot deeper if you

hadn't followed her to the end of the driveway." Sage drew a deep breath. "We stepped in it, brother. We're in hip-deep shit. Let's search your rental, and then we'll get the fuck out of here."

Bear checked to make sure she was inside the vehicle before he closed the door. "Where are we going?"

"Bienvenu. It's where I live, and if we're followed, I'll know."

Bear took one last look at Piper. The poor woman had been through it tonight. "You want to bring whatever this is to where you live?"

"It's the safest place I know." Sage took out his phone and turned on the flashlight. "I'll search the vehicle; you stay with her.

"I need to get her meds." She'd said she needed them to go to another college. He couldn't imagine what the events of tonight had done to her.

"We'll have to have Guardian work their magic. Once she wakes up and tells us what she's taking, Guardian can get with a doctor and call in a prescription." Sage scooted around the front of his vehicle as Bear grabbed his phone and went to the rear. He turned on the flashlight and started the search.

"Got one." Bear reached up and pried the

magnet-backed tracker off the vehicle's under-carriage.

"Make that two," Sage said, grunting as he fought to release the magnet.

Bear swore silently and kept looking. "They had to put these on before they firebombed the house."

"With all the electronic doorbells in this neighborhood, CCS should be able to find some recording that shows what happened."

Bear looked at him since they were both under the vehicle searching for trackers. "Don't they need a warrant for that?"

"I'm not in the lawyer business," Sage said as he slid farther under the truck. "Son of a bitch. Look at this. Number three."

Bear moved farther under the vehicle and sighed as he spotted another one. "Four." He searched after he pried it loose. "Check inside the fenders." Even though they were fiberglass, they could have taped one in.

"Good call." Sage scooted out at the same time he did. They searched the vehicle again and then called it. Four trackers. Four. Overkill much? What in the hell was going on?

He turned the devices around in his fingers.

"High-tech. Small." About a quarter of the size of one of the round trackers people put in their suitcases.

Sage took the trackers from him and tossed all four onto the ground. "When they don't see us move, they'll come looking. Let me get you that weapon you asked for."

Bear waited for Sage to come back. He took the case, opened it, and pulled out the forty-five-caliber automatic. After inserting a clip and chambering a round, he dug out the holster and clipped it to his jeans. He tossed the case in the back seat, slid his weapon into the holster, and turned to Sage. "I'll follow you." Bear got into the rental and backed out of the driveway. He pulled in behind Sage. It was time to get the fuck out of Baton Rouge.

Piper slept for a while before she jerked several times before waking with a start. Bear put his hand on her arm. "It's all right. We're not in Baton Rouge any longer."

She sat up, her head on a swivel. "What happened?" She dropped her head to her hands. "I hyperventilated."

"And passed out. Do you know what type of medication you need? We can get you a refill."

He saw her nod and figured he'd shut his mouth while she sorted out things. She found the remote at the side of the seat and lifted the back upright. "I don't know if I can do this." Her words were soft, and she was looking out the passenger side window.

Bear understood. Being shot at, firebombed, and almost run over in the course of an hour was rather extreme. He wasn't sure who was being shot at when they were hugging the asphalt, but he'd count that as the second murder attempt with bullets that night. "I understand. We're going somewhere safe. We can work on the documents and determine what's going on."

"I need to be at the school tomorrow." Piper's foot started tapping rapidly on the floorboard of the rental.

"Because that's your routine."

"Yes, and I have classes I need to teach." She turned to look at him. "I can't lose my teaching assistant job. I won't be able to afford my rent or tuition for the program."

"Guardian will ensure your employers know it isn't your choice."

"I work for a department."

Bear nodded. "I stand corrected. I promise you

that you won't lose your job for helping us." Bear had seen Guardian move mountains. That was a tiny issue for the organization to fix, especially since she was the only one who could read Topher's notes.

Piper was silent for a long time. "We're heading east."

"We are," Bear acknowledged.

"How long was I out?"

"Not too long. I think your body and mind needed to reboot. Like it did when we were sitting in the driveway."

"I don't know how I fell asleep." She let her head drop back on the headrest. "I've never done that before. Fallen asleep so suddenly like that."

"It's a stress response. People handle it differently. I was in a hostage situation once, and one of the captives slept through almost everything." Bear shrugged. "We thought he was dead, and the hostage takers were lying to us. But he was alive and well, just asleep."

Piper's foot stopped tapping, and she turned to look at him. "What do you *do* for Guardian?"

"I'm a part-time employee. I'm called up when needed." He hit his blinker to pass a car going way too slow in the fast lane.

Piper started rocking back and forth in her seat. "That's not what I asked."

"Are you okay?" Bear put his hand on her back, and she stopped rocking. He slid it up and rubbed her neck, trying not to notice the thick, soft silkiness of her hair as it moved against the back of his hand. She shivered a bit, and he wanted to stop the car and hold her until she could sort out her feelings, but that was way out of context, and it wasn't his job. But it didn't stop him from wanting to do it. Instead, he offered her words of comfort. "There's nothing to be afraid of now."

Piper huffed. "That isn't how the panic attacks work. There can be nothing happening. Nothing going on, and I'll end up on the floor of my closet with the door shut, freaking out and terrified of ... something."

"The medication helps?" Bear continued to message her neck with his fingers.

"It does, but I don't like to take it. I feel like I'm moving in glue." She leaned back into his hand. "I don't let anyone touch me." Bear didn't say anything. He kept up the soft pressure. Her neck was delicate, but her muscles were so tight he could only imagine the stress she was dealing with. "This is why Christopher lets you call him Topher."

Bear chuckled. "This being what?"

Piper sighed and closed her eyes. "Whatever magic you're doing now."

He wasn't doing magic; he was trying to give her something to hold onto. Contact with another human was what he'd need if he'd freaked the fuck out. No judgment, no trying to talk him down, just knowing the person was there. Yeah, he'd want silent support. "Is it helping?"

"Yes, well, this, and you haven't told me to stop freaking out." She chuckled. "My dad has done that my entire life. He told me I was exaggerating. He'd yell at me to grow up, to stop acting like a baby. Believe me, if I could stop the attacks from happening, I would."

"I do believe you." Bear felt the muscles of her neck start to relax a bit. It sounded like Topher and Piper's dad was a wicked tool. He abandoned Topher and verbally abused Piper. Bear considered the two options and decided maybe Topher got the better end of the stick. Topher didn't have to live with his father's toxicity. But his thoughts weren't important. The critical thing now was to get Piper her meds. "What type of medication do you use?"

Piper told him the name and the dosage, and when Bear stopped his massage, Piper sighed in complaint. He hit Sage's speed dial and waited for the man to answer. "Everything all right?"

"Yes." Bear relayed the name of the medication and the dosage to Sage.

"I'm going to call Doc Wheeler directly. He shouldn't be asleep yet. I'll see what he wants to do. Do you have her doctor's information?"

"Piper, who's your doctor?"

She rattled off the name. "He's the college's doctor."

Bear started to relate the information, but Sage cut him off. "I've got it. Standby."

He hung up the phone and glanced back at Piper, who was sitting back against the seat. There was no space for his hand, so he took the hint. His phone rang a few minutes later, and he didn't recognize the number. Bear answered it.

"This is Dr. Wheeler. I work with Guardian. May I speak to Piper Whitehead?"

"She's right here." Bear handed the phone to Piper.

"Hello?"

Bear listened to the conversation from Piper's side. Every now and then, he could make out the doctor's side of the conversation.

"I fell asleep after we got out of the fire. I

haven't done that before." Piper started chewing on her thumbnail. Bear wanted to reach over and place his hand on her arm, removing the nail from her teeth. But he didn't know how she'd react, so he left it alone.

"That's what Bear said. Stress." She looked over at him and gave a quick, almost-there smile.

The conversation lasted for about a half hour. They were working their way through the heart of New Orleans on I-10 when she hung up. "He's impressive."

Bear glanced over at her, his ire up just a bit at the admiration in her voice. And boy, did that slap him in the face. He needed to get a grip on his protective instincts. Why they were out of kilter was beyond him. He gave himself a mental ass-kicking and asked what she meant. "How so?"

She shrugged. "I've been seeing a doctor for my anxiety. Yours knew what he was talking about and what questions to ask."

Oh. Okay, so, no need to go caveman. Good to know. "Is he going to prescribe something?"

"Yes. A single dose until he can call my doctor tomorrow. He said it was my decision whether or not to take it, but he recommended I stay on a lower dose at all times instead of taking them occasionally. He was going to talk to my doctor about that." Piper closed her eyes. "Is Christopher alive?"

Bear sighed. He wouldn't lie to the woman, and even though she'd had one hell of a night, he would tell her the truth. "I don't know, Piper. I swear to God, I don't know."

She nodded and turned her head to look out the window. "He needs to be."

Bear didn't say a word. His gut told him Piper was going to need her medication.

CHAPTER 6

Piper woke with a start. She sat up in bed and glanced around. "Oh," she said. She was at Sage Browning's house. His fiancée, Honor, had given her the pajamas she now wore. Piper blinked at the shutters and the sun that streamed in. What time was it? She twisted and looked for a clock. Nothing. Her phone sat on the bedside table. She picked it up and looked at the time. It was almost ten o'clock in the morning. Sighing, she pushed her hair back out of her face.

A soft knock on the bedroom door spun her. "Just a minute." She pulled the blankets up over her. "Come in."

Honor poked her head around the door. "I thought I'd bring you a few things." She sat a basket down just inside the door. "Shampoo, conditioner, a comb, toothbrush, toothpaste, and a change of clothes. I think we're about the same size, you're thinner, but my clothes should work until we can wash yours."

"Thank you. Is Bear ..."

"He and Sage are in the office working on the documents. They have been since about six this morning. One of our friends, Beau, stopped by with clothes for Bear before he went to work. Nothing Sage had would fit." Honor laughed. "I have coffee and a small breakfast waiting for you. The shower is through there."

Piper nodded. "Thank you. I'll be out soon."

"Take your time." Honor gave her a quick wave and left, shutting the door behind her.

Piper got out of bed and, with the basket in tow, went through the process of washing the smell of smoke off her. She leaned against the back shower wall and relived what had happened in the past twenty-four hours. The documents were the key to discovering where Christopher was and why he was missing.

She got out of the shower, combed and braided her wet hair, dressed, and emerged ten minutes later. She found Honor in the kitchen with a laptop. "Hey. Coffee, cup, creamer, and sugar are on the counter. There's a fruit and yogurt parfait in the fridge."

Honor talked to her as she typed, and Piper stared at her. "How do you do that?"

Honor stopped typing. "Do what?"

"Type and talk at the same time?"

Honor laughed. "Oh, after eons of doing my job, you'd be amazed how proficient you can become at doing two things simultaneously."

Piper started to ask what job she did but stopped as she assumed it wasn't her business. She went to the fridge and retrieved the parfait. Small chunks of apple and walnuts alternated with yogurt. Piper took the spoon from the glass and sampled the yogurt. Plain. Thank goodness. She sampled the apples and walnuts—a bit of cinnamon but no sugar. "Oh, man, this is good," Piper said as she ate.

"Thank you. I'm trying to learn how to eat healthily. I was always overweight. Recently I lost a lot of that weight, and I want to keep trim but do it in a healthy way." Honor looked at her as she spoke while typing. Piper didn't think she'd ever get used to that.

"Thank you for the clothes, by the way. They fit perfectly."

"How do you stay so trim?" Honor asked.

"Oh, I run marathons, so healthy is the only way I eat."

Honor blinked and stopped typing. "Is it hard? Running a marathon?"

Piper took another bite as she considered the answer. "At the beginning, the training and gaining the experience with the miles? Yes, it takes discipline, and it helps if you dedicate the time to building a routine. That's what I love about it, knowing how many miles I'll run on any given day. Then when you build up to a certain level, it becomes more of a mind game. Your body settles into a rhythm, and your mind can start to play tricks on you."

Honor took a sip of her coffee. "What kind of tricks?"

"It may tell you that you can't go on, but you have to power through that. Experience is the best teacher of that lesson." Piper took another spoonful of yogurt. "What are you doing?"

"Oh, running a criminal background check for one of the Guardian investigators in California."

"From your kitchen table?"

Honor chuckled. "I usually do it from the office, but I don't have the clearance to look at the documents they're going through. So, today, I'm couch surfing and enjoying the change of location."

"I'm so sorry if I inconvenienced you." Piper scraped the last of the yogurt out of the cup.

"You didn't. If I had something important to work on, I'd drive into the office in New Orleans, but today is just routine requests. We're caught up for the first time in what seems like forever." Honor pointed to a cabinet. "Filtered water is in the fridge in the pitcher, and there are glasses up there. Bear and Sage said to tell you to come in once you had breakfast."

"Thanks." Piper filled a large glass and drank half of it. Refilling it to full, she popped open the top of the pitcher, added more tap water, and put it back into the fridge. That was a routine for her. She shut the fridge and picked up the glass. Her skin prickled on her arms. Piper felt something had shifted. She turned around.

Bear leaned against a column that marked the kitchen from the front room. "Good morning. I like the clothes."

Piper glanced down at the yoga pants and t-shirt that said Witness Protection Program on it. Honor laughed. "That shirt was purchased for me as a joke. I'm passing it along."

"Thank you again," Piper said to her before turning her attention to Bear. "I'm sorry I slept so late."

Bear shook his head. "I'm not. You needed to recharge. Yesterday was a hell of a day."

Piper drew a deep breath. "That's an understatement. Did you find anything?"

"La, la, la, la ..." Honor put her hands over her ears. "Not authorized to hear."

Piper laughed at the antics. Bear nodded to the office, and she followed him with her glass of water in hand.

They entered the office, and Sage looked up from a computer. "Hey, good morning."

"Hi."

Bear pulled out a chair for her, and she sat down. Piper swiveled so she could see him. "What have you found?"

Bear sat beside her, a stack of papers in front of him. "Not a hell of a lot. It's mostly puzzle pieces, and we don't know how to fit them together, but we did get permission to read you in on the information you need to know about all of this, including our Cuban mission. We also received some information on Christopher."

"What?" She jumped and hit her water glass. Bear snatched the glass. Only a small amount of water dropped onto the table. The speed of his reaction was unbelievable. "How did you?"

Bear swiped the water away from the paperwork. "Lucky, I guess. Christopher went to DC." He showed her a notepad with the flight number, airline name, and date.

"That's the same day he told me he was going out of town and would be back when I returned from Caltech."

Bear nodded. "He booked a round-trip ticket. He didn't get on the plane to return to Louisiana. Guardian is dispatching people to the hotel where he is registered. There are charges on his credit card. Every three days, so …"

"He's renewing the reservation?" Piper smiled and grabbed Bear's arm.

"Maybe." Bear nodded, but he didn't look as excited as she was.

"What aren't you telling me?"

"He had a rental vehicle. It wasn't returned. The rental agency considered it stolen. They found it at the hotel and retrieved it. Topher hasn't called the company or the police to report it missing." Bear put his hand on hers. "We're waiting for a call from Guardian now. In the meantime, we're sorting all these documents, looking for something to help us in case we need to go to DC. We can have them as a reference and work them as necessary."

Piper nodded, and her foot started tapping. She put her thumb to her mouth, but Bear stopped her. "Dr. Wheeler had this delivered this morning. He spoke with your doctor, and they agreed that taking one of these every day until things return to normal was the best course of action due to the stress in the situation. If you want to talk, both are willing to speak to you." Bear put a small brown vial in front of her, and she glanced at the label. The dosage was smaller, but not by much. She prayed a lower dose could stave off another panic attack and not make her feel like a sloth while the rest of the world was stuck on hyperspeed. She opened the bottle, popped one in her mouth, and downed it with water.

"Where are the notebooks?" she asked, ready to get started.

"Right here."

"I had a thought in the shower. I should start with his most recent notes. Right?"

Sage lifted his head from where he was running documents through a high-speed scanner. Bear handed her both of the books. "Absolutely. Read backward from the time closest to his disappearance."

She took the bottom book and opened the back pages. The last entries in the book were about a report. "Do we have a FOIA report from something called the DIA?"

"Defense Intelligence Agency," Bear and Sage said at the same time.

Bear continued, "It's the military equivalent of the CIA."

Sage typed on the keyboard. "So far, we have seven on the inventory list. I think I just saw one. But which stack?"

"May I see what you have?" Piper stood up and moved over Sage's shoulder.

"Here, you take this stack and I'll grab the other." Sage got up, and Piper slid into his seat.

She glanced at the notebook again. "What is hummit?"

Bear frowned. "Could you mean H-U-M-I-N-T?" He spelled out the acronym.

"Yes, that's what he has." Piper looked at her brother's shorthand.

"It means human intelligence." Sage came back with another stack of papers and started rifling through them. "Here it is. This is the one I remember. There may be more, but this one is the one I saw."

Piper ran her finger under her brother's writing and read, *"Talk to Dr. Franklin about the DIA refused report. Is HUMINT incorrect? Report E1 incorrect?"*

"Dr. Franklin," Bear said as Sage reached for his phone. "A name to start with." He glanced a Sage who nodded, putting his phone to his ear.

Piper watched as Sage spoke to whoever was at the other end of the phone. "All right." He hung up. "They're working it."

"What's before that in the notes?" Bear asked her.

Piper flipped the page backward and chuckled. "He's hungry." She skimmed down the page. "Here's the next entry, not talking about pasta. But it's just a bunch of letters listed in a row."

"What are the letters?" Bear asked.

"DIA. That's the defense agency, right?"

"Correct." Sage nodded.

"MIB?"

Bear pointed at Sage, who'd opened his mouth to speak. "Not the movie."

Sage blinked. "Then I have no idea."

Bear chuckled, "Me either. We can hit the search engines. Next?"

"NGIA."

The phone rang before anyone could talk. Sage picked it up and listened, glancing at Piper and then at Bear. "I got it. Thanks." He put the phone down. "The hotel said that Christopher called and authorized them to keep charging his room and that he needed to extend his stay. That was two days after he arrived. The maids said he hadn't returned. His personal belongings are at the hotel."

Piper leaned back in her chair and clutched her brother's notebook. "He's not all right, is he?"

"We don't know that yet," Sage said.

Piper looked at Bear. "Don't lie to me. Tell me the truth. I need to know."

Bear glanced at Sage. "It isn't looking good, Piper. But don't give up hope. Topher needs us to keep digging."

She stood up, still clutching the notebook to her chest. "I need some air."

Sage lifted, but Bear stood. "I'll go with her."

She didn't care. She walked through the living

room, still clutching the notebook. Bear got to the front door before she did. She went onto the wide porch and sat on the top stair. "He's gone, isn't he?"

"I hope not," Bear said as he sat beside her. She started rocking back and forth. A self-soothing habit she'd developed early in life. Bear's hand landed on the back of her neck, and that soft pressure started again as he rubbed the tight muscles. Piper felt her heart breaking. Christopher was her protector, confidant, and best friend. Even the mere thought of him not being alive tore a jagged hole in her chest. She didn't have enough memories of him. They didn't have enough time together. He couldn't be gone. No, she couldn't accept what she feared to be true. She took a deep breath and then another.

She closed her eyes. "I'm sorry."

"For what?" Bear asked as he continued to massage her neck softly.

"For being like this. For not being able to deal."

"You've dealt just fine. No one thrust into your position could have handled it any better."

"I want to go to DC. I want to see the hotel room. To see his things. I want to be closer to him."

"I can arrange that." Bear continued in that rhythmic motion. Piper dropped her head and noticed the notebook. She dropped the book to her lap and opened it from the back. "After the list of letters, NGIA, NSA, CCS, NRO, DCISA. He wrote: *Conspiracy? U-235 missing, agencies using E-1 cover?*"

She stared at his handwriting and flipped the page backward. "*Double talk, redirection. No linear progression. When all else fails, solve for X.*"

"What does that mean? Not only the solve for X comment but the numbers. too." Bear's hand was still rubbing her neck.

She stared at the notebook. "I have no idea what E-1 is. 235 is uranium. Low reactor-grade uranium. U-238 is the naturally occurring uranium that isn't fissile and can't start or sustain a nuclear reaction. I need to identify where the problem started. The first article is about the warehouse in Venezuela. That is what's going to tell us what's going on. All this tracing of the documents began or ended at that article."

"Can the uranium he's talking about be used in weapons?" Bear's hand moved in a steady squeeze, release motion. He must have felt the shiver running down her spine at the question.

"Weapon grade uranium is expensive and difficult to make. It needs an enrichment of ninety percent. The majority of uranium that is unaccounted for is reactor-grade and fissile. So, it can be used for things like dirty bombs, yes."

Bear sighed, and he shook his head. "The fire screwed us. We're missing a lot of documents."

She flipped the page backward. "No, we're not." She pointed to the page. "A synopsis of each requested report with dates of request and the agencies response." She turned the page backward again. "Here. This is a report he requested from the Freedom of Information Act. Look, he wrote out the FOIA information that is at the bottom of the request. This looks like a stamp, like the one on the other documents in the office." She pointed to the little diagram he'd drawn. "He circled it." She flipped the page and pointed to the same thing again. "And down here, and he circled it again." She paged back and back. "Circled again." She flipped through the pages. "Here, he says, *the office that directed the exemption of this report stated E1.*" She looked at Bear. He was staring at the river.

"What's E1? That's the second time it was mentioned, right?"

Piper shook her head. "At least. I haven't seen anything like a key that would tell me what it is. It might have something to do with the request itself. Maybe?"

Bear shook his head. "I don't know, but I know people who would. It's little enough to go on."

"But we have the starting point and these pages with the document synopsis. That's enough, isn't it? He figured it out. We can, too."

Bear stared at her for a long minute, his hand resting on her back at the nape of her neck. "Are you sure you're physically ready for what we might find in DC?"

Piper shook her head slowly. "No, I'm not. But I know I wouldn't forgive myself if I didn't try." She closed the book and turned to him. "I know two people in this world who make me feel safe. Christopher is one of them."

Bear's hand slipped from her neck when she moved, and he leaned back on the porch using both arms to support his muscled upper body. He was so big, and she would normally be terrified of a man his size.

"Who is the second?"

"You." Piper dropped her eyes. "You make me feel safe. I don't know why, but you do."

She sent a glance in his direction. He was staring at her. "I know that sounds stupid."

He sat up and leaned forward, his elbows on his knees as he looked at her. "It doesn't make you sound stupid. I'm sure you're sensing something that tells you I'm not a threat to you. I can be intimidating, and I know that, but it's not always a bad thing. My past training and experience make me uniquely able to protect you. In my line of business, you learn to trust your instincts, and I'm glad you're trusting yours."

Piper felt relief wash over her. For some reason, what Bear thought was important to her. It probably had to do with the fact that he'd stayed with her through an epic meltdown and hadn't belittled or chided her for what she couldn't control. "What are your instincts telling you about Christopher?"

"That he's in deep trouble." Bear sighed. He reached over and grabbed her hand, threading his fingers through hers. "They're also telling me that we need to stay together in order to get to the bottom of whatever is going on. As a team, we can work through the information Christopher left for us, and we'll find out what is going on. Together, we can deal with the good, the bad, and the ugly because there *will* be bad, and there *will* be ugly, Piper."

She stared at the hand that held hers before lifting her gaze. She was terrified of the bad and the ugly, but when she looked at Bear and saw his calm confidence, she swallowed hard and nodded. “I can do it.” She prayed that it wasn’t a lie.

CHAPTER 7

Bear entered the office and shut the door behind him, so he and Sage could make their call. Piper wasn't included, but she'd accepted she wasn't cleared to hear some information. Instead she sat in the kitchen transcribing Topher's notes as she waited. Honor had driven up to New Orleans to buy clothes for him and Piper.

"Ready?" Sage asked as he sat down.

"Let's do it." Bear listened as Sage checked into the conference call.

"Sage, what have you got going on?" Bear recognized the voice as Jared King.

"Sir, I have Bear with me."

"I copy. CCS is online, too. Let's have the scoop."

"Bear, you take it." Sage gave him the green light.

"The day before yesterday, I received a call from Piper Whitehead, the half-sister of Christopher Whitehead. He wasn't home when she returned from a business trip, which was unusual. She became worried and, after some time, called me."

"Why you?" Jared asked.

"Topher and I were tight in Cuba. We've texted back and forth since then. I called once or twice. Topher told Piper to call me if she thought something had happened to him." Bear glanced over at Sage, who was staring at the speakerphone, not him.

"All right. CCS, give me a rundown on the players," Jared asked the people who Bear hadn't heard until that point.

A male answered, "Christopher Whitehead, a former consultant for the …" Bear listened as they ran down Topher's positions and education. They switched to Piper and listed her education and current status, which validated everything she'd told Bear.

"My people in DC tell me he's missing from the hotel. His belongings are still in the room, including a cell phone."

"What about a computer?" Bear asked.

"No mention of a computer on the inventory list."

"Piper said his computer was missing. His personal computer."

"Does she know what's on it?"

"No, but based on what we found in the house, I'd say a backup to the notes he'd taken, or perhaps the notes were a backup to the computer." Bear shrugged, although no one but Sage could see him.

"And what have you found in the notes?" Jared asked.

Sage took that question. "It's a work in progress. Piper is the only one who can read his shorthand, and she's transcribing, but those notebooks are thick. It'll take time."

"She understands what he's writing and has the education to make sense of what he says," Jared spoke as if thinking out loud, so Bear didn't respond. "Listen, I'll put this as plainly as I can. None of the agencies that Christopher worked with are concerned about his disappearance."

Bear frowned and leaned forward. "Excuse me?"

"I know. It's beyond me, too. I'm giving the intel I received. None of the agencies he consulted or worked with considered his potentially missing status a blow to their security. What was relayed to me was that it has been so long since he worked for them that any information he may have known is now outdated and useless."

"And Guardian?" Bear waited. He couldn't imagine turning it over to the local police departments to work.

"Guardian looks after its people, even if they're independent contractors. Bear, you and Ms. Whitehead need to go to DC. Have her continue deciphering those notes. Con, tell them what you have regarding Dr. Whitehead's movements in DC."

"Roger that, sir. We have him exiting the flight that he took to Dulles. He took an Uber, which was confirmed through his credit card, straight to his hotel. That night he ate at a restaurant within walking distance from the hotel. We searched for Dr. Franklin as requested. There are far too many in the DC area, so I applied a filter to remove all MDs, DOs, chiropractors, and all doctors of known medical specialties, then searched the remaining pool of people for physicists. There was one. He's currently on staff at the DIA and works as a consultant for the NSA. I cross-referenced the time Dr. Whitehead was working with the NSA to the time of Dr. Franklin's employment, and they worked at the agency at the same time. I can confirm that Dr. Whitehead had an appointment at the DIA the next morning. He Ubered from the hotel to the DIA, checked in at ten-twenty-two in the morning, signed through security, and was escorted out of my view. I assume he was a good little government trained minion and arrived early for his appointment, so it would be logical to assume it was at ten-thirty. He departed the facility at ten-thirty-seven."

"Con, I'm not going to ask how you know those details." Jared sighed.

"Nothing that would get us in trouble. I hacked into the unsecured camera system across the street and watched him enter at ten-twenty-two, validated by the rideshare's charge on his credit card. Dr. Whitehead stopped at the desk—I assume to sign in—and a member of the military, who was at the front desk, took him out of camera sight. At ten-thirty-seven, he reappeared and exited the facility."

Bear rubbed his chin. "Only seven minutes? Did he have a computer with him?"

"I don't know. He did have a messenger bag, so it's conceivable. But the DIA would have searched it and made him surrender it until he left. They're particular about signal security."

"Where did he go from there?" Sage prompted the man Jared had called Con.

"To a rental car agency. From the rental agreement in his room, he rented a car for two days. The rental agency declared it stolen five days after it was due back. Alexandria police found the vehicle in the parking lot, notified the rental agency, and it was towed."

"And no one thought to ask in the hotel about Dr. Whitehead?" Bear looked at Sage, who shrugged.

"The police weren't looking for a missing person. They were looking for a missing car." Jared said. "Dr. Franklin is your starting point, Bear."

"I'm not an investigator." His work was more along the lines of kicking ass. He left the niceties of the mission to others.

"But you have the most knowledge of Christopher and understand Ms. Whitehead. From the information I received from Dr. Wheeler, she could be a considerable hindrance should she not be able to cope."

"She has her medication. She'll be all right," Bear defended Piper because she wasn't in the room to do so for herself.

"Good. As far as not being an investigator, we've got that covered. Con is on tap to complete all digital forensics. When you land, you'll be met at the airport by one of ours with what you'll need. You'll have access to one of my best investigators, twenty-four-seven, if you need to talk something through or need confirmation that you're on the right trail. She'll be there for you. I'd rather keep her on the case she's currently working, but if necessary, I'll pull her to help you."

Bear rolled his shoulders. All right, he'd go with the role he'd been given. "Between us, Piper and I should be able to piece together the information in the notebooks. If we need help, I'll make the call."

"Con, make the arrangements."

"On it."

"Bear, for your information, we've canvassed all the morgues in the area. No John Doe matching

Christopher's description has been brought in. Do you need anything else?"

"No, sir." His shoulders relaxed a bit. That was a good sign, but it also only meant that if Christopher was dead, no one had found his body yet.

"Good luck on this one. Something is off. I wish I could be out there in the field with you."

Bear chuffed, "I wish you were, too. It's been more than a few years since Cuba, but I bet your interrogation technique hasn't suffered."

Jared laughed. "That wasn't an interrogation, my friend. I was being nice."

"Tell that to Mariella's uncle." Bear chuckled.

"Nah, he's not talking to me right now, and that's a good thing. Find our man. Whatever it takes."

"As long as it takes," Bear answered Jared, and the phone disconnected.

"You need help out there you call me," Sage said from the other side of the table.

"I will. I'm not a fool and won't mess this up by not asking for help."

"What's the first step?"

"We get as much inventoried and scanned in as possible while we're here and work on transcribing his notes when we're done. Then Piper and I start putting the puzzle pieces together. We start with Dr. Franklin. As far as we know, he was the last person to talk with Topher before he disappeared."

"The rental agency," Sage supplied.

"We'll go there, too." Maybe Topher left something in the car.

"How else can we track him?" Sage sighed and picked up a redacted report. "What was he after?"

"It has something to do with uranium."

Sage's head popped up. "How do you know that?"

"Guessing based on Topher's notes."

"That could be ugly with a capital U, my friend. I thought we were done following the radioactive trail when we left Cuba."

Bear shook his head. "It seems we aren't. I don't think Topher let it go when we left Cuba."

"What are you talking about?" Sage leaned forward.

"There was an article from a Venezuelan newspaper dated three days after we floated out of Cuba. It warned the remote area residents to stay out of a warehouse that the police had raided as it was radioactive."

He watched as Sage realized what he'd said.

"You don't think there were two operations to make those fucking bombs, do you? One in Cuba and one in Venezuela?"

"As far as I know, we never found the people responsible for the bombs." Bear spread his hands and placed them on the table. "What if Topher kept looking?"

Sage scrubbed his face with his hand and sighed. "The next time we call in to Guardian, we need to let them know what you just told me. Jared will have all the information on that mission and what it did and didn't reveal."

Bear nodded. "When we get our travel arrangements, I'll tell them about my hunch." Topher wasn't happy with the outcome of their time in Cuba. He'd said as much on several occasions and wanted to press on to find out how to take down the bad guys. Only how did you topple the Cuban government?

Bear leaned back in his chair. "I wonder what the political environment of Venezuela was then?"

Sage opened up the computer and typed something. "Not good. Not good for a long time. Economically, socially, or politically. It would make sense to have a second operation in the works."

"Which would be vacated immediately when the operation in Cuba was disrupted."

"Put on mothballs until the heat is tolerable or gone," Sage agreed.

"But it's been years, and there's been no threat of dirty bombs. The build-up to our Cuban mission was considerable and obvious."

"Granted." Sage looked at the door and leaned in a bit. "But the Fates were running that show. What if someone else has control now and is considering utilizing the dirty bombs for another tactic or strategy? Something totally different."

Bear followed Sage's thought process. It made sense, but fuck him, they couldn't prove one damn bit of the suspicion. "We're spitballing without facts."

Sage nodded. "Then go get us some facts, my friend."

Bear stood and extended a hand, pulling Sage out of the chair that time. "Whatever it takes."

When he walked out into the kitchen, Piper looked up at him expectantly. "No news. Just plans on getting us to DC, so we can try to follow in Topher's footsteps. Anything new there?"

She deflated and looked down at the paper she was working with. "No, that Freedom of Information act stamp is annotated repeatedly, but he doesn't say why."

"FOIA. It's easier to say." He pronounced it Foy-yah. "That's what we called it in the military."

"FOIA," she echoed his wording and nodded. "Everyone has their version of shorthand, don't they?"

"The military is great about making acronyms." Bear sat down beside her. "Are there any differences in the stamps?" Bear looked at his notes.

"Yes, each organization lists a responsible office, and then, there are these letters. I'm assuming, and I could be wrong, that these stamps are utilized like a library with first-edition or only-edition works. But that's applying my logic to his research without the proper background. I don't know if I'm correct."

"We can find out. We'll be going to the DIA to talk with Dr. Franklin. We can ask at the DIA what they are." For some reason, his hand went to the back of her neck and massaged the area again. *Yeah, he had no idea why. Maybe he was possessed by a touchy-feely teenage boy or something.* Or he'd fallen under the little bird's spell. She was beautiful and appeared delicate and fragile, but she was a marathon runner, so she was stronger than most women. He considered her akin to the China his mom had in the cabinet when he was growing up. He had to be extremely careful when near it, or he could break the beautiful, thin porcelain. Yet he'd seen a cup fall to the ground without breaking. Only a small chip was removed from the rim. He'd never felt so compelled to ensure a person was pulled together and protected from the outside world. He didn't want Piper to chip. He wanted to protect her from the cracks that life caused in people's lives.

Piper looked up at him and smiled. "I don't know why, but I like it when you do that."

He smiled. "If I ever overstep, if you don't want me to do this or anything else, you say no. I don't want to make you feel uncomfortable."

She closed her eyes and leaned back into his grip. "I know that." She opened one eye and looked at him. "At least I know it now. You scared me at first."

Bear chuckled. "On the drive to Topher's house, I thought you would tap a hole in the rental's floorboards."

She chuckled and smiled softly, closing her eye and relaxing back into his grip. "I didn't know you.

I only knew that Christopher trusted you. You could have been an ax murderer."

The way she looked at him when she opened the door to Topher's apartment, he thought she'd already convinced herself of that fact. "Surprise, I'm not."

"Thankfully." She smiled and then sighed. "My anxiety is manageable, mostly. But I feel more in control when I follow my routines. Christopher going missing wasn't routine. You weren't routine. My anxiety was already pushing to the point where I should have medicated, and then everything happened. I like to know what's happening and when."

"You've said that before. Why do you think that is?" Bear worked the muscles of her neck as he spoke.

"You mean my fondness of routines? My doctor said that the need for a schedule comes from when I was growing up." She shrugged and settled her shoulders. "My father wasn't exactly dependable."

"So, if tomorrow morning I tell you what's going to happen and about when it will happen, at least for tomorrow's events, you'd be better able to deal with the day?" He could certainly do that. If it made her life easier, he could give her a straw man of what he expected to happen.

Piper opened both eyes and turned her head. He stopped rubbing her neck and waited. "It would help."

"Then that's what we'll do."

CHAPTER 8

Piper looked at the paper in her hand for the thousandth time. She'd memorized the schedule, but having it in her hand was an added comfort. They'd already driven to New Orleans. Both she and Bear had a suitcase of new clothes, thanks to Honor. They processed through security and were waiting at their gate. They'd fly to DC next and be met by someone from Guardian.

Bear's arm was over the back of her chair. She welcomed the protection from the people behind her who were jostling about and generally being obnoxious. Piper held her new courier bag on her lap. Inside the bag was her link to Christopher. She'd been unable to sleep last night and ended up praying. She knew religion. She'd been raised in the church. Her father ensured she was, but she'd never been religious. The facts and theory didn't always mesh in her mind. But last night, she fell back into the comfort of her childhood beliefs. She'd needed a higher power. She'd needed an omnipotent being with an all-knowing presence, an entity that knew the beginning and the end, with whom she could whisper her fears and ask for help. She'd needed the comfort of knowing that while not everything may turn out how she wanted, there was a purpose in her days. A purpose in Christopher's days.

"Piper? We're boarding." She jumped when Bear spoke.

"Sorry." She stood up with him, and they made their way to the front of the long line of people waiting to board. They walked down the long tunnel to the aircraft and were seated in first class. Piper put her bag on the floor in front of her and buckled in. They sat quietly as the plane filled, and when the aircraft taxied out, she gripped the armrests tightly. Bear reached over and covered her hand with his. She inverted her hand, and he threaded his fingers through hers.

She should be embarrassed. Most people flew

without issue. She wasn't like most people. She hated flying. "We'll level out soon." Bear's comment came through the rattling and jiggling of the aircraft. "Are you afraid of flying?"

She turned to him. "Afraid? No, I don't like it. Somehow, this machine is supposed to stay in one piece while traveling through the atmosphere. Yes, as a physics major, I understand the science. I understand the extraordinary safety of the air industry, but that doesn't change the fact that I am —or will shortly be—traveling at over two hundred miles an hour at an altitude of thirty-thousand feet above the ground. Any crack in the structural integrity of this aircraft, and we are bloody ice cubes falling to the ground."

The lady across from them in the aisle seat bent forward and looked at her. Had she spoken that loud? The lady lifted her hand when the fasten seatbelt sign went on. "Another vodka and cranberry juice, please."

Bear turned toward her and smiled. "I think someone else agrees with you."

Piper closed her eyes and dropped her head back on the seat. "I said that too loud."

Bear leaned over. "No, she's just listening too closely."

Piper laughed. “Better not talk about anything important, then.”

“Until she falls asleep or passes out.” The attendant walked down the aisle with the woman’s drink.

“Where’s home for you?” Bear asked her, and his thumb rubbed her hand where their fingers intertwined.

“Baton Rouge,” she answered and then realized what he meant. “Oh, I grew up in Saginaw, Michigan. What about you?”

“I grew up in Katy, Texas.” Bear shrugged. “My parents moved after I entered the service. When they passed, I got out on a hardship discharge and moved to a small town in northern Utah, where they lived with my brother. I opened a gym, sold the semi my father and mother owned, and put my brother through college.”

“Are you still there? In that small town?”

“Yes and no. I have a business there, but I also have three other locations. I normally spend a year or two at the latest opening, helping it grow to ensure the people I hire know my standards. Once that’s done, I pull up stakes, find a new location, and start a new gym. I didn’t start out to grow the business that way, but it seems to work.

What about your parents? Are they still in Saginaw?"

"My mom is. My dad died a year after I moved to Baton Rouge. I won't go back, and she won't come to Baton Rouge."

"Why's that?"

"Because of Christopher. She has never been able to accept the fact that Dad had an entirely different family that she didn't know about. She *forgave* my dad for not telling her, but she didn't want anything to do with Christopher. Out of sight, out of mind."

"Ostrich much?" Bear chuckled.

"Exactly." Piper agreed with him. "Did you go to college or straight into the military?"

"I joined after I graduated high school. That's when I got involved in martial arts. My instructor told me that being able to kick … ah … butt wasn't the only thing I should know. He suggested I go to school at night. I did. The military paid for my bachelor's degree in business."

"Do you miss it? The military?" She lifted a hand. "I'm sorry. I'm being rude. I shouldn't ask so many questions."

Bear's brow furrowed. "You're not being rude. Why would you think that?"

Piper stopped herself from saying why. "I just didn't want to seem pushy."

"You're anything but pushy. Honestly, you remind me of a timid bird."

"A bird?" She looked up at him. "Is that an insult?" Was he making fun of her? Why a bird?

He shook his head slowly while staring at her. "No, imagine a beautiful bird sitting in your hand, and a loud noise happens. The bird flies away and disappears, afraid of the noise, although it couldn't hurt her. You remind me of that bird in a way. The noise of the world scares you, but instead of flying away, you're still resting in my hand and trusting me to take care of you. You've resisted the temptation to fly away. You're a warrior, my little dove."

Piper stared at him. He didn't seem to be making fun of her. She lifted her eyebrows. "A warrior dove is an oxymoron."

Bear laughed. "Point taken, but it's true in your case. I bet your heart is racing a million miles an hour, yet here you are, pushing forward."

She stared at the man next to her. "How do you see me?" No one had ever been able to understand her. Well, no one but Christopher, and even he had moments of frustration with her. He was good at hiding it, but she could tell.

Bear cocked his head. "I'm not sure what you mean?"

She broke eye contact with him and stared at the back of the seat in front of her. "How …" She shook her head. "Christopher said when you look at someone, you don't always see who they are. They wear masks. Everyone wears masks." She looked at him again. "How do you see through to who I am?"

Bear looked down to where their hands were linked. "I've done a lot that has fine-tuned my ability to judge a person. In some instances, it's saved my life. I see you because, unlike other people, *you let me see you.*"

"I do?" She hadn't made that decision. "How?"

"When you were overwhelmed two nights ago. You came to me, and you were raw. You bared your soul to me, looking for help. How could I not see who you were?" Bear lifted her hand in his. "I've never had another human bare themselves and be completely open to me. You made an impression. One I'll never forget." He pressed his lips to the back of her hand. "I swear I'll take care of you, my little dove. No matter what happens when we land, no matter where the road goes in this investigation, I will protect you, and I will be there whenever you need me."

Piper stared at the man, transfixed by his words and the searching stare that locked with her gaze. She felt him lean forward, and she licked her lips. He was going to kiss her.

"Would you care for a snack?" Piper jumped when a basket of junk food appeared in front of them.

Piper grimaced at the selection. "No, thank you."

"Do you have any fruit?" Bear asked the attendant, still holding her hand.

"We do have some bananas and apples." The woman smiled at him.

Bear looked at her. "What would you like?"

Piper considered the question for less than a second. "Banana, please."

"Two bananas and two apples, please." Bear turned to her. "If you don't eat the apple, you can take it. We aren't flying into another country, so hanging on to the fruit isn't a crime."

"A crime?" She may have squeaked that question.

Bear nodded. "You have to declare any fruits or vegetables that you bring into the country, and most of the time, it's confiscated because it has to undergo a rigorous inspection process."

"How do you know this?" Piper thanked the attendant who brought back the fruit. Bear let go of her hand so she could take it.

Bear laughed. "I'm full of useless information, but in this instance, I watched a customs agent in Miami jack up a seventy-year-old woman for trying to bring an orange into the country. It was very enlightening."

"Did you intervene? You did, didn't you?" Piper peeled the banana as she asked.

Bear raised an eyebrow. "I did, but why would you assume that?"

"Because you wouldn't let an old woman be afraid or accosted." She broke off a piece of the banana. "Am I right?"

Bear smiled and took a bite of his apple. Piper laughed and popped the banana into her mouth. She realized she saw Bear, too, because when she'd come to him for help in that moment of utter despair, he'd shown his true self: the caretaker, the man who would protect a defenseless woman. Bear was a modern-day gentleman—kind in a way she hadn't often seen.

She finished her fruit, both pieces, and leaned

back as she watched the attendants do a ballet with the passengers moving around in the first-class cabin. She'd never traveled first class. Bear messed with the screen in the seat in front of him. A diagram of where they were in the flight path came up on the screen. "We have about three hours," he noted.

She nodded and reached for her new carrier pouch, taking out a new notebook Honor had given her yesterday and the one she was transcribing.

"Do you still think the X in this equation is the first article?" Bear leaned over.

Piper glanced at the woman across the aisle. She was wearing a headset and watching a movie. She glanced up at Bear. "I do. But …"

"But what?" Bear shifted, so he was turned on his hip facing her, completely shielding her and the conversation from anyone.

She shook her head. "I'm having doubts. Are we going the wrong way?"

Bear's chin shifted, and his brow scrunched a bit. "You'll have to explain that."

"If that article is the beginning, is going backward on his research the right way to look at this problem? We might miss something that we didn't know about. Something key to whatever sent him to DC."

"I'll defer to you on that. Do you think we're missing something?"

She nodded, thumbed back two pages, and pointed to another annotation of the FOIA response. "Why is it circled? I want to go back and find the reason he's doing this. If we can figure out why he's focused on it, we'll have something."

"Then do it." Bear reached down and grabbed the bag. He lifted out Christopher's other notebook and added it to the one she had in front of her. "Be a genius." He winked at her.

"I'm far from that." She'd had her IQ tested. Her intelligence was high but not as high as some.

Bear settled back in his chair and crossed his arms. "I call it like I see it." He smiled and closed his eyes. Piper took a moment to stare at his profile. His short brown hair looked so soft that she wanted to reach up and run her fingers through it.

Piper shook her head and opened the notebook before her, although she wasn't reading the words Christopher had put on the page. She was thinking about Bear and what kissing him would be like. To have him hold her. The men in her life had been colleagues who were academics. Sex, when she'd had it, was lackluster and disappointing. She understood the science behind sexual arousal and climaxing, but obviously, something was missing from the equation for her. Her partners had climaxed, but she hadn't. She was the common denominator, so the deficit had to be hers. It was a puzzling conundrum.

She continued to stare at the book without seeing it as her mind wandered to what sex with Bear would be like. His hands were rough and callused, yet they were so gentle. He could easily smother her with his size, but that wasn't how she saw him. He was careful with her. She leaned her head back and closed her eyes for a moment. How would it feel? What about his size in *other* areas?

Piper's eyes popped open. *No, no, no*. Imagining Bear's personal areas was out of bounds.

"Everything okay?" Bear asked without opening his eyes.

She nodded. "Fine, fine. I was just lost in thought for a moment." When he didn't open his eyes, she let hers drop down his chest to his crossed, muscled arms and onto his jeans and the bulge there.

Piper glanced up and froze. Bear was watching

her check him out. Her cheeks instantly heated with the warmth of a thousand suns. She jerked and quickly grabbed her brother's book. *Oh, Lord, I won't be able to look at him again.*

Bear shifted and leaned toward her. "A penny for your thoughts?"

She shook her head. "Nothing. I was just … Nothing." Her cheeks were now in a nuclear meltdown. She pulled her scrunchie out of her hair and let it down so it would act as a drape between them.

His hand landed on the back of her neck. It set off a shudder through her body that she couldn't control. The sensations growing between her legs were new and very distracting. She squeezed her legs together and pretended to read the words on the page, flipping it even though she wasn't registering a word.

Bear took his hand away a few moments later. Piper flipped the notebook back to the beginning and started to read. She read for at least a half hour before she saw it. Piper stopped reading and reached out to touch Bear's leg. "He wrote you a note."

"What?" Bear bent over. His face was beside hers. "What does it say."

Piper looked up and around them. She glanced over at Bear. "Not here."

He nodded and leaned back in his seat. Piper read the page again. *Oh, Christopher, why did you start this?*

CHAPTER 9

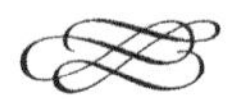

Bear was certain Piper had been checking him out. The blush that immediately blossomed told him he was right. And that shudder when he touched her told him that she wanted him. *Right back at you, babe.* She ticked every box he liked. *Athletic.* Check. *Smart.* Check, in bold, with a highlighted emphasis. *Sexy as fuck.* That one got him. She was pretty and seemed fragile, and God, it turned his crank even though it shouldn't. He shouldn't be thinking of how attracted he was to his little dove. She was a mission. Scratch that. She was his partner on the mission. He didn't mix business and pleasure.

He dropped his hand from her neck. Then again, most of his missions were of the male-only type of company, so he didn't have a basis for that line in the sand, did he?

Piper reached over and touched his leg. Not in a sexy I want to get to know you type of way, but it immediately caught his attention. He leaned toward her. She told him Christopher had left him a note in the first book. He glanced at the date on the top of the page that Piper had indicated. The date was about a month after they'd returned from Cuba, almost seven—or was it eight—years ago now. God, what could Christopher have to say to him? He thrashed through his memories to find anything but came up empty.

Their meal was served, but Piper shook her head and kept working. He ate his food and asked for more fruit for Piper. He watched as she worked and ate. The notebook cover shielded her notes. He drew a deep breath and leaned back in the seat. When he first joined the mission to Cuba, he'd assumed it was a quick infiltration. In and out. But when the mission was briefed, he knew instinctively that keeping Topher alive was his mission. The guy was mentally tough, but he wasn't a warfighter. The constant changes and adaptations of the mission were hard on Topher. Bear knew from experience that not all embedded people in a military mission could cope, so he took Topher under his wing and made sure the man had the information and felt valuable during the portions he had nothing to do. He liked Topher. They had absolutely zero in common, but he liked the guy. Topher had a hell of a sense of humor. Granted, most of it was highbrow shit, but it was funny, especially with the dry way Topher delivered the lines. He was kicking himself now for not reaching out more often.

But communication was a two-way street, and he and Topher had drifted apart. There wasn't any deciding point on that happening. It just happened.

The announcement that they were landing was finally made. Piper continued to work until the attendant asked her to put the table away. Piper ignored the woman. Bear put his hand on her leg, and she jumped. He immediately placed his hand on the nape of her neck. "Sorry. We're landing. They want you to put your table up."

"Oh." Piper blinked and then looked at the notebooks. She scrambled to close the books and lift the table at the same time, dropping the notebooks in the process.

Bear leaned forward and placed his other hand on her leg. "Piper, you have time. Slow down."

"I'm sorry," she said as she bent down to retrieve the books after finally securing her table to the back of the seat in front of her. "Sorry."

"There's nothing to be sorry for. You were concentrating and didn't hear."

She nodded and opened her courier bag. "He ..." She glanced around. "I need to talk to you. He was doing this for a reason."

"I'm sure he was," Bear said as they tightened their seatbelts. Topher wasn't the type of person to run off on tangents. He was methodical when it came to his life. His belief on that point was validated at his apartment and his mother's home. Everything on the wall had been annotated in the notebooks and probably on Topher's computer. His office? Bear couldn't explain that mess, but that was the exception, not the rule, for the man. Maybe the office was Topher's junk drawer.

They landed and were one of the first to deplane. Bear guided them to the luggage claim, where he also found the Guardian, who was there to give them the equipment that Jared had promised.

"Colten McCallister. Whatever it takes, brother." The man offered his hand.

"As long as it takes. Bear McGowen, this is Piper."

The man shook his hand and nodded to Piper. "I have some things for you and your vehicle. Follow me, please."

"Did you see his badge? Do you know he's a Guardian?" Piper whispered to him as they followed Colten through the throngs of people heading toward the parking garage exit.

"I know he's Guardian." He was also a Marine in a previous life. The tattoo that was visible on the man's arm confirmed that fact. Additionally, the man was packing. Discreet and stowed away, but he was carrying a firearm.

"How?"

Bear smiled down at her. The woman was terrified. He stopped walking and put both hands on her shoulders. "I know. I'm not going to let anything bad happen to you. I will protect you. Do you believe me?"

She stared up at him and owlishly blinked once and then again. "I believe *you* think so."

He chuckled. "I have the skills and the qualifications to do everything I've promised you. I don't think so; I know it."

Her gaze stayed connected to his for a long moment. She finally nodded. "I believe you."

"Good." He turned and looked for their escort. The man was waiting patiently by the door. As they approached, his fellow Guardian gave him a look as if saying, "Is everything okay?"

Bear gave the guy a nod, and the man turned on his heel and led them to a black SUV. "This is yours." He tossed Bear the keys. "Standard equipment. Personal weapon in the console. Your reservations are in the glove box, and Dom Ops requested that you check in as soon as you get settled."

"Thanks." Bear shook the Guardian's hand and watched him jog over to an identical SUV and enter. He watched the man pull out of the garage and clicked the key fob for the back end to open up. Bear knew a small armory of weapons was under the carpet flap, but Piper didn't need that information. It might spike her anxiety, and he didn't want that to happen. He put their bags into the rear and shut the door.

Bear walked her to the passenger side, opened the door, and helped her in. Not because she couldn't get in by herself, but because he'd promised, twice now, that he'd be there for her protection. That was him, giving her that reassurance.

He shut the door and jogged to the driver's side after she was in. "He said there was a weapon in here." Piper held very still as she spoke.

"There is. Have you ever been around weapons?"

She shook her head. "My father had a gun, but I couldn't touch it."

"Ah, well, when we get to the hotel room, I'll make sure it's safe and unloaded, and then I'll let you take a look at it." He put the vehicle in reverse and backed out of the parking garage. "Would you get the reservations out of the glove box and get us directions to the hotel?"

Piper did what he asked and plugged the address into the GPS on her phone. "I watched coverage of the explosion that took down Guardian's building. It was tragic. So much loss."

Bear nodded. "Bad men doing bad things. There's a lot of that going on in the world." Guardian existed to try to right the balance of good versus evil. He was positive the organization would be active for many lifetimes to come.

"Oh! The note. Let me get it." She pulled out the

notebook and opened it to the page she needed. Bear waited as she found the spot.

"Here it is."

Bear, if you are reading this, my suppositions have been proven as more than mere guesses. My sister, Piper, is reading this to you, or Guardian has somehow broken the code of my shorthand. I hope it is the former rather than the latter. Piper will be able to help you follow my logic and my notes. She is the best thing to happen to me in a long time.

"He loves you," Bear said when Piper stopped momentarily.

"I know. He knows I love him, too." She took a deep breath and continued reading.

When we tracked down the items in Cuba, a female was mentioned. Do you remember? The men at the warehouse mentioned her when they were in the back of the truck with us. It came up again at the out brief. Mr. King mentioned it and asked if I knew or suspected anything else about manufacturing the dirty bombs. We went through each day, each conversation. That comment the builders made about the woman when we were in the back of the truck stuck in my head. An American woman with a black passport.

I haven't been able to rest. I feel compelled to find out how. Who and why is irrelevant and are null points as the players will most certainly change. A diplomatic passport would mean official government involvement. But which government agency? I'll leave that to people who are better equipped for investigations.

The 'how' is where my expertise lies and where I'm starting. To build weapons, one must have the material. That is where I'll start. I have duplicated my note-taking in case either the journals or my computer goes missing. You said you'd make a warrior of me, I guess this problem is my sword, and I will find out how to wield it.

Piper turned in her seat and paused when the GPS on her phone directed him to an exit. She continued after he exited. "Solve for X when Christopher started his search was to try to identify where the radioactive material that contaminated the warehouse in Venezuela had come from."

She flipped the page. "He started pulling other

articles at that point. They, too, indicated contamination due to uranium. The levels he guessed at by using national health statistics for each country. Here on this page ..." She flipped to the other notebook and moved toward the back of the book. "He'd annotated ... here." She stopped at the page she was looking for and skimmed along with her finger. "*Noting the instance of acute radiation poisoning indicated in the Venezuelan documentation that is now public for that year, I can say with certainty, whatever was in that warehouse was not reactor grade, but more than likely weapon grade uranium.*"

Bear shook his head. "But it hasn't surfaced since it moved from the warehouse. And the government would have tracked it. That is an international nightmare. The news and political mayhem surrounding weapon grade uranium being unaccounted for and out in the world would be unprecedented." And the information she gave him was way over his pay grade. He'd contact Jared as soon as they checked in.

Piper made a distracted noise and kept skimming as she talked, "Hasn't it surfaced? We don't know that yet. Christopher wrote that weapon grade material is strictly controlled." She closed the book and thought for a moment. "The Iranians have been trying for years to make enriched uranium. They're capable of enriching to twenty percent now. What if the material in Venezuela was brought in from the former Soviet Union or a country like Iran working toward the capability? It doesn't have to be ninety percent to cause radiation poisoning, especially with extended proximity to the material." Piper rubbed her head as she shook it. "The truth is reporting for countries who have signed a non-proliferation agreement can be inspected. Countries like North Korea and Iran? I don't know the protocol, but I hope people from this country are monitoring what's being done."

Bear knew for a fact that one or more organizations were probably assigned that nasty little detail. There were ways to gather the information. Infiltration would be rare, but monitoring movement, communications, and satellite surveillance all came together to give the United States a damn good idea of what was happening.

As he followed the prompt on the GPS, Piper fell into silence, lost in thought, as was he. He pulled into the hotel's parking lot and drove into a parking slot. "Ready?" She nodded and started to open the door. "Hold on." Bear grabbed the small case from the console and popped the back hatch of the SUV. He put the gun in the bag and secured the back before he went to her door and opened it. He used his free hand to help her down.

Bear opened the lobby door for her, and they walked to the desk. "Reservation for McGowen."

"Yes, sir, I have a room with two king-sized beds."

"A single room?" Piper asked. She glanced up at him, her eyes as big as silver dollars.

"Yes, ma'am," the clerk said. "Do you want it to remain on the corporate card it was reserved under?"

"Yes, please." Guardian paid for all the lodging on his trips. He hadn't even thought about giving the woman his credit card.

"Would you like to leave a credit card for incidentals or place that on the corporate card as well? May I see your IDs, please?"

"Leave it as is." Bear said. The clerk stopped typing, glanced at each ID as they flashed them, and then slid two plastic key cards through the machine to code them. "There's free wi-fi, and the restaurant is open until nine tonight. The bar stays open until midnight. Breakfast is served from 6 a.m. to 10 a.m. Can I get you anything else?"

"No, thank you." Bear accepted the card, and they walked to the first-floor room. Guardian's doing again, no doubt.

"We should have separate rooms," Piper said as she walked into the room.

Bear shut the door and put down the bags. "If we were in separate rooms, how would I protect you?"

Piper spun at his question. "From what?"

Bear rubbed the back of his neck and tried to connect the dots for her in a way that wouldn't cause her anxiety to spike. "We know Christopher is in trouble, right?"

She nodded.

"Someone broke into your apartment, tried to run you over, and shot at you. You were the only one visible from the front window. I was still at the table. You were moving toward the sink, passing the window."

Piper blinked as her arms straightened, and the bag on her shoulder slid to the floor with a thud. "Why would someone want me dead?"

"You can read Christopher's work."

She glanced down at the bag on the floor. "They don't want it to be read."

"That's my assumption."

Piper nodded and then looked up at him. "I'll be back." She went into the bathroom and shut the door. The next logical step in that train of thought was that they didn't want anyone to have it, which meant Christopher was probably dead. Bear didn't want to say it, and Piper most certainly didn't want to hear it, but the truth was an ugly bitch.

Bear sighed and pulled out his phone, dialing the number he'd been instructed to call.

"Operator Two-Seven-Four, how may I direct your call?"

"This is Bear McGowen. I was told to call Dom Ops."

"Yes, sir, Mr. King is waiting for your call. Hold, please."

Bear sat down on the edge of the bed.

"Are you alone?" The question was Jared King's greeting.

"Semi." He glanced at the closed door.

"A body washed up on the shore just under the Woodrow Wilson Memorial Bridge in Alexandria. The description matches Christopher Whitehead."

"Shit."

"Yeah."

"Cause?"

"Drowning is the initial guess, which, given

what I know about Whitehead, is a load of shit. The man competed in Ironman competitions."

"Where?"

"I'll send directions. Either you or his sister will have to make an identification. The body didn't have anything on him when he was brought in."

"All right. I take it this case will be elevated on the priority list?"

"It's already at the highest level here at Guardian. As I said before, none of the other agencies felt that his disappearance warranted any concern." Jared sighed. "What in the hell was he doing?"

Bear saw the bathroom door open. Piper leaned on the door jamb and looked at him. "Piper found a note to me in his first journal. Piper, would you come here and read the note to Mr. King?" He put the phone on speaker.

She went to the floor and grabbed the notebook out of the pouch. She moved over to where he was sitting at the foot of the bed and sat beside him. Piper read the words verbatim, and Bear capsulized their conversation about the material.

"There are organizations that do nothing but track materials like this. Why didn't Dr. Whitehead go to them?" Jared asked after Bear was finished.

"He did." Piper swiped at the pages. "He was told he didn't have … what was it … an official reason or acting in an official capacity. Therefore, he didn't have the need to know and that unless there was an agency inquiry about a specific shipment, they wouldn't release any information about the movements or location of weapons-grade materials."

Jared swore. "This gets more convoluted as we go."

"That it does," Bear agreed.

"I'll send someone over, and then tomorrow morning, if Piper feels up to it, we'll have an all-call and discuss the next move."

"Why wouldn't I feel like it? Why are you sending someone over? Where are you going? It's about Christopher, isn't it?" Piper's eyes grew wide.

Bear grimaced. She was too damn smart for her own good. "I'll call you back."

"Roger. Dom Ops out." Jared disconnected.

"I need to go out."

"Where?"

"The morgue."

"They found him? He's dead?" Her words were the faintest of whispers, and she was pale. Her brown eyes were huge as she looked at him, pleading for it not to be true.

He put his arm around her and spoke as he pulled her into his side. "They don't know if it's Topher. There was no ID."

"I should be the one," she said and stood, moving away from his touch. "I'm the only family he has. I need to be the one. I need to see him, to know for sure." She picked up the bag and put the book inside. "Let's go."

Bear tried to talk her out of it, "Piper, you don't have to do this. I can go."

She turned around and lifted her chin. "Yes, I do, and you're going with me."

She opened the door and walked out. Bear grabbed his key card from the dresser where he'd tossed it and jogged out after her. When he caught up, he pulled out his phone and called Jared asking him to send the address. They were in the SUV and moving less than a minute later. Piper hadn't said another word.

CHAPTER 10

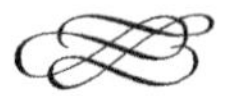

It was as if Piper was watching herself move. The building was low and gray, and the lights in the parking lot were starting to turn on. Bear walked beside her, and she knew he was worried about her. She wished she could tell him she was all right and would make it through the experience without a meltdown, but she couldn't.

She had to be the one to identify him. She was sure he would've done the same for her. Christopher had been her best friend and mentor. He deserved so much more than that. After Bear rang the bell at the front door, a muffled voice came through the speaker. Bear told them why they were there and that he was with Guardian. A metallic click sounded, and Bear opened the door.

Piper stared at the floor. Tan tile. Matte finish. The walls were white, and two security guards were behind the tall desk. She stood by Bear as he spoke and filled in paperwork. Then they were moving. Her mouth was dry, and her stomach hurt with a pain that defied physical boundaries.

Their footsteps echoed in the empty hall even though other people were walking in the building. She was acutely aware of the sounds of her and Bear's footsteps. They were shown into a room with four chairs and a window. There was a curtain outside the window, not the inside. The rationale avoided her momentarily, and then it came to her. It was on the other side, so the person showing her the body could close it.

As she stood beside Bear, he put his arm around her and stood with her. Not telling her to sit down, not making small talk, not asking anything from her, and for that, she was grateful. She barely held on to her bravado in the hotel room. It was her mask. It was her needing privacy and respect from not only Bear but also the rest of the world.

The door opened again. "Mr. McGowen, Ms.

Whitehead. I'm Sergeant O'Neil. My job is to ensure the law is followed and identification is confirmed."

Piper just stared at the man. He was in his fifties, balding a bit, with a gray mustache and red hair. The difference was striking and unusual.

"Are you ready?" Bear's question drew her gaze away from the officer. She turned toward the window. *Was she ready? No, she'd never be ready. No. No, she wasn't.* Piper nodded her head and stared at the white curtains that were on the other side the glass. She focused on the glass as the officer pushed a button on the wall. The clear window had wires laced through it. Why? Who would want to break into the …

The curtain moved, and a body, covered in a white sheet, lay just past the window. Piper stepped forward and placed her hand on the cool glass. She stared at the silver that was exposed around the drape of the sheet. It looked so cold.

The attendant reached up and lowered the drape.

Piper swayed against the glass. *Oh, God. No.* She stared at her brother. There were cuts and gashes all over him. His face was swollen and disfigured under the damage, his lips blue and his skin white.

So white. His hair had been pushed back to expose his face. Piper could feel the tears falling. She could feel the scream rolling up her throat. She knew the sound ripped out of her came from the depths of her soul. She couldn't hear it, though. She couldn't hear the scream. She couldn't focus on anything except the sight of her brother. *Christopher. Oh, dear God, no. Christopher!*

Piper screamed again when the curtains started to shut. She pounded on the glass, demanding the man open it again. She slammed her fists against the window. There was no pain. There was nothing except the gut-wrenching knowledge that Christopher had been killed. He'd been beaten. *She needed to see him again. She had to tell him she loved him. She needed ... she needed ... to breathe ...*

BEAR HAD her in his arms when she went limp. He moved her for a better grip. "Sir, I'm sorry, but I need verbal confirmation." The officer looked down at his clipboard.

"That is Dr. Christopher Whitehead. He was a friend and her brother."

"Yes, sir. We have smelling salts, and I can get the EMT from the back if you'd like."

"No. I know how to handle situations like this. How do I arrange to get him home?"

The man pulled several sheets from the clipboard. "If you have any questions after you read this, you can call the number at the bottom of the page."

Bear extended his hand, and the officer put the paper in his hand. "I'm sorry for your loss, sir. And for hers."

"Thanks." Bear knew the guy was only doing his job. "Can you grab her bag for me?" He motioned to the floor where the courier bag lay by the window.

The officer bent down and picked it up. He placed it in Bear's hand. "I'll get the door."

"Thank you," he repeated and walked down the long hallway. Piper had been so strong, but the sight of Christopher, of what had been done to him, was almost too much for Bear. It was no wonder she'd lost it. He waited for the front door to open before hip-checking it and carrying Piper to the SUV. Opening it and getting her inside was an exercise, but he managed. He got behind the wheel, checked on her again, and called Jared King.

"Go," the man said as a way of greeting.

"It was him. He'd been beaten, probably tortured. Don't let the county do the autopsy. If he was killed, he found something. Something that someone didn't want him to share."

"I'll have our people pick him up immediately. How is his sister."

Bear looked over at the woman next to him. "Not good. Not good at all."

"I'll give you time. Call me tomorrow when you can."

Bear disconnected and debated driving back to the hotel or waiting. She jerked, and he decided to wait. It took a couple more minutes, but she woke. Only that time, she didn't sit up. Her eyes opened, and she blinked, then looked up at him. "They hurt him."

"They'll pay. I swear, they'll pay." He reached over and moved the hair from her face. "I'm going to take us back to the room now."

She nodded and closed her eyes. The soft crying as he drove through Alexandria gutted him. The pain Piper was feeling carved out his heart. But not with a sharp knife. No, this was more like amputation via a dull spoon. There was nothing he could do. No way to make it better. No way to protect her from the pain.

But he would ensure whoever did that to Topher, to his friend, would get worse. He gripped the steering wheel so hard that it should have his grip as a permanent impression.

He didn't have to tell her to wait when they pulled into the hotel parking lot. He opened her door and slung the courier bag over his shoulder. "Can you walk?"

She nodded and got down out of the SUV with his help. He reached for her hand, and they walked back into the hotel together. He opened the door, and she went straight into the bathroom. The shower came on. He went to the door and listened as Piper cried. Who did that to him? He couldn't give a flying fuck about the materials or the rest of Christopher's investigation. At that point, finding out who ordered Christopher's beating and death was paramount, and he couldn't do that without Piper's help. Only, she wasn't in any condition to do that. Not then, and maybe not ever.

Bear waited twenty minutes before knocking on the door. There was no answer. He opened the door slightly and saw her in the shower. He shut the door, went to her bag, and got out underwear, but he didn't see anything resembling pajamas. Opening his bag, he put a t-shirt under the clean panties and her toothbrush and toothpaste. He turned to the bathroom door before he remembered to grab her comb. As he was going back to the bag, the bathroom door opened.

Piper was wrapped in a towel and standing in a cloud of steam. Her wet hair hung over her delicate shoulders. Bear froze with her clothes in his hand. "I thought you might need these."

Piper sniffed and extended a hand. "I can't get the shower to shut off."

Bear handed her the clothes and went into the bathroom. The lever was stuck, and it took a quick jerk with some muscle before he could turn it off.

He walked back out as she dropped his t-shirt over her head. He turned and went back into the bathroom. He'd be happy to look at that perfectly toned body at any other time, but not that night. Not when she was grieving. He waited for a minute before coming out. She was under the covers, curled in a ball, turned away from the door with the covers pulled up to her ears. Only the top of her head was visible.

"I'm here if you need me."

She nodded her head up and down, acknowledging his words. He ensured the door was locked. Bear grabbed his weapon case, which he'd forgotten about on the jog after Piper earlier, and a pair of boxers and headed into the shower.

As soon as the door shut, he opened the weapons case, checked the chamber of the forty-five automatic, and then slapped in a magazine. He pulled back the receiver group to chamber a round and sat the weapon on the counter beside the shower stall. The shower was one of the fastest in his life, and considering his time in the military, that said a lot. He soaped up, rinsed off, and got out. The water stuck on again. He shoved it into the off position. He'd report that in the morning. Right then, it wasn't a concern. Piper was.

After toweling off, he pulled on his boxers and grabbed his weapon before leaving the bathroom. Then he rechecked the doors and went to his bed. He sat on the edge and stared at her. "Are you asleep?"

"No." She turned to look at him. "Would you hold me? Please? I can't stop shaking."

Bear moved over to her bed and lay beside her while staying on the blankets. She turned to face him, and he pulled her closer, keeping the blankets wrapped around her. She sighed but didn't say anything. He placed his hand on the back of her neck and just held her. He had no words of comfort, no platitudes. They were useless.

He knew when she finally fell asleep. He didn't move, not wanting to wake her. Instead, he closed his eyes, and with the ability gained from missions of the past, he slept.

CHAPTER 11

Bear quietly closed the hotel room door again. Piper had moved away from him during the night, so he'd moved to his bed for a couple more hours of sleep. After waking up in the early morning, he'd gone to the restaurant for coffee, taking something back for Piper, although she probably wouldn't eat.

He stepped outside of the hotel and called Jared.

"How is she?"

"Sleeping. Do we have anything on Topher yet?"

"He was tortured. Eight of his fingernails had been removed. There were shards of wood under his toenails. Our ME just started the autopsy, but the visual exam confirmed he'd been worked over."

"Jesus. What did he fall into?"

"I don't know. Can you make a meeting? I'm in Alexandria for the week. I want to get you here, so we can work a plan for going forward."

Bear glanced back at the hotel. "How long? I don't want to leave her. She could be in jeopardy. Hell, someone's tried to kill her twice. The shots at Christopher's house could only be aimed at her. I wasn't visible, and then the vehicle tried to run her over."

"My concern also. I'll send some people to watch the room and area while you're gone."

"I'll wait until they get here. In the meantime, I need to make arrangements for Topher."

"I figured you would. I'll have you back by noon. We'll talk about arrangements when you get here." Jared sighed. "Nothing makes sense with this one."

"One thing does, sir. Christopher is dead, and whoever killed him wants to eliminate Piper, so he must have told them she could read his notes." Bear leaned against his Guardian-supplied SUV.

"That's more than likely the only concrete thing

in this whole damn mess," Jared agreed. "I'll let you know when our people are in position."

"Thank you."

Bear went back into the hotel and into the room. He sat down and penned a note for Piper. When he received a text telling him people were on scene, he folded the paper, wrote Piper's name, and left the room quietly. Colten was leaning against the wall. "I got her. You take care of business."

"Thank you," he said and headed straight to his SUV. It took him thirty minutes to get to the address on his GPS. He pulled up in front of a huge old house with a realtor for sale sign in the front yard. Jared King stepped out of the front door wearing jeans and a polo. Bear got out of the truck and went to the porch. "Nice office."

"I've been working from home since the Siege, but we're transitioning to a new house." Jared opened the front door. Bear walked in and noticed the dark, rich woods that stood out from the beige-colored walls. The dark brown oversized couches and chairs still looked small in the massive room. He waited for Jared, who led him to the kitchen, which was brightly lit and modern, the exact opposite of the living area. The cabinets' granite, rich wood tones, and a center island the size of his entire kitchen were impressive.

Jared pointed to a seating area past the kitchen. "We'll meet in there. Coffee?"

Bear shook his head. "No, thanks. I had a cup this morning."

"Only one?" The voice startled him, and Bear jumped. "Up here." The man's voice called his attention to the television on the wall. "I'm Con. We met."

Bear narrowed his eyes and cocked his head. "And you are on the television, how?"

Jared chuckled. "I asked my sister that the first time she popped into my house uninvited."

"I was invited." Con crossed his arms.

"You were. Is everyone else online?"

"Not yet. We're waiting on Archangel. Do you want me to patch them through or wait?"

"Wait until everyone is here, please." Jared sat with a cup of coffee, and the television screen went dark.

Bear blinked and looked at Jared. "Archangel is involved?"

Jared nodded. "Yes, he's involved anytime we lose one of ours."

"Topher was a contractor, like me. We aren't

Guardian unless we're on a mission."

Jared shook his head. "Not true. Whether you're on the payroll full-time or not, you're our assets."

Con appeared on the screen again, but a patchwork of squares was populated that time. "Archangel is online."

"Everyone, this is Bear McGowen. Bear, at the top right, is Archangel. Bottom right is Con, who you've met. The top left is Nic DeMarco, who works at Dom Ops with me, and on the bottom left is Tori King, my sister-in-law. She's our liaison to all the intelligence communities in the Beltway." He indicated a beautiful blonde in the corner. She looked up and smiled before returning to whatever she was reading.

"Beltway?" Bear hadn't heard that term before.

"The greater DC area," the woman said, still looking down.

Jared leaned back in his seat. "Is everyone up to date?"

"I'm just now reading the report." She looked up. "How is Dr. Whitehead's sister?"

"Distraught. She suffers from extreme anxiety as it is. Last night, identifying her brother, in the state he was in, was traumatic." Bear suddenly realized he hadn't reminded her to take her medication. Fuck, that was on him. He'd make sure she took it if she hadn't remembered. He glanced at his watch, hoping he'd make it back before she woke up.

"I'm looking at the background. Do we know what Dr. Whitehead was talking to Dr. Franklin about?" Tori flipped a piece of paper and leaned forward before she started typing. "He's been with the DIA for quite some time. Did they know each other?"

"Yes," Con said before Bear could. "They worked together."

"But you said the meeting only took seven minutes total." Bear leaned forward. "It couldn't have been a pleasant meeting. They didn't linger and play catch-up."

"Tori, find out what you can about what programs within the DIA Dr. Franklin is currently working on." That came from Archangel. The man leaned forward.

"I'll do what I can. The DIA will resist and give me the runaround. They always do."

Jason sighed and took off his glasses. "I want movement on this situation. What can we do to make the discovery go faster?"

Con spoke, "If I could work with Dr. Whitehead's sister, I can make a key for his shorthand. We can digitize his notebooks, and a computer can decipher the good doctor's work in far less time than it would take to transcribe by longhand. She'd need to validate the transcriptions, however. Programs that turn handwritten documents into digitized formats are not perfect."

"How long would that take?" Archangel asked.

Con narrowed his eyes. "If I can get Brando to take some of these priority requests, I can do it in short order. But I need a key, and we'd need to get her to a secure location to digitize the notebooks."

The man introduced as Nic asked, "What do you mean by a key?"

Con shifted his gaze and answered, "Something already transcribed. A page or two so most of the alphabet or characters used for words can be identified."

"She's transcribed enough of the material from those books to give you a key. We're trying to follow his rationale, but we haven't been able to connect the dots." Bear pushed his hand through his hair. "Honestly, my priority now is Piper. She's been attacked twice. Her apartment has been broken into. We need to get her somewhere safe, so she can work on the documents. Plus, she needs to bury her brother."

"Guardian will take care of all costs associated with the funeral." Archangel laid that statement out there before continuing. "We'll take care of sending him back to Baton Rouge. If Piper can tell us where she wants him interred, we will make it happen."

"Thank you, sir. She's in a doctoral program. I don't think she has much money."

"She'll have Dr. Whitehead's insurance money," Con said as he typed. "Three policies for a million each taken out ... Yep, right after he returned from the Cuba mission, which was the last time he worked for Guardian. He changed the beneficiary from the university to Piper three years ago." Con kept typing as he spoke.

"Back to the point about her protection. Bear, I don't have anyone more qualified than you in that category. The location is what we need to determine. Someplace where you two will be off the grid and still be available to answer questions about the transcription and work on the case using Dr. Whitehead's logic. We need Piper to follow her brother's research. We have the brightest and the best working for us, but none of them are physicists, nor do they understand Christopher as she did."

Jared leaned forward. "I can think of three places like that. One is closer than the other two."

Archangel leaned back. "I don't want to assume the occupants would be amenable to visitors."

"I'll call and ask," Tori said. "Until we know who tortured Dr. Whitehead, why they want his research destroyed, and why they've tried to kill Piper, she needs to be off the grid. Whoever is behind this is willing to kill. She has a target on her back until we have this solved."

"Is there anyone they can get to who may be used to blackmail her out of seclusion?" Nic asked.

Bear nodded. "Her mother. She lives in Saginaw, Michigan."

Jared nodded. "We can handle that. Nic, contact the northern district and have them put a protective net around Piper Whitehead's mother."

"Consider it done."

"In the meantime, Con, get whatever you need together to work with Piper on this transcription."

"I have most of it, I'll need to write some code, and we'll have to encrypt it, but that's a matter of keystrokes." The man seemed confident in his ability.

"Tori, work some magic on the DIA."

"I'll do my best. But I think going through the parent would be easier and more beneficial."

"The parent?" Bear was lost on that one.

"The civilian in charge of the organization. In this case, it would be the Under Secretary of Defense for Intelligence and Security." She talked as she typed. "Jason, you'd have better luck with the political appointees, but I'll work it through my agency contacts, too."

"Agreed. I'll make the call. What else do we need to know from the DIA?" Archangel looked up expectantly.

"We need to know what the meeting between Dr. Franklin and Dr. Whitehead was about. I want to do that interview myself." Jared leaned forward. "I'll be here until the end of the week."

"He'll be at your disposal by the end of the day," Archangel growled. "Bear, we'll sort out the location where you'll take Piper. Be ready to go. We don't want you in this town any longer than necessary."

"We haven't unpacked."

"Good. Take care of her. Please pass on our sincerest condolences. It doesn't mean shit right now, but they're genuine. Make sure she knows we'll take care of Christopher, make all notifications to the insurance companies and his employer, and get whoever killed him. That's a personal promise from me to her."

"Yes, sir. I'll let her know."

The call ended, and Jared stood. "We won't let this go unanswered."

Bear stood, too. "Thank you." He extended his hand.

Jared grasped it firmly. "Whatever it takes."

"For as long as it takes," Bear answered. He glanced at the clock on the wall. "I need to get back."

"Then go, and Bear?"

"Yes, sir?"

"If possible, you'll be in on the takedown."

Bear felt a sneer spread across his face. "I'd appreciate that, sir."

* * *

PIPER WOKE WITH A START. Her head ached, and her sinuses felt clogged. She opened her eyes and blinked, trying to … "No," she groaned when the memories of last night dropped on her. The weight of the thoughts crushed her, making it hard to breathe.

Sitting up, she looked for Bear. He'd held her last night until she went to sleep, but he wasn't there now. A piece of paper, tented with her name on it, caught her attention. Sighing, she pushed the blanket off and dropped her head to her hands as she tried to breathe. But how did one focus on such insignificant details when their world shattered into a million pieces?

What would she do now? How would she go forward? She needed to bury Christopher. Sniffing back tears, she shook her head. How would she do that? She had no money. Piper lifted her head and stared at the phone on the small desk in the room. She could call her mom. Her mother *could* help, but she *wouldn't*. Maybe a loan? No, all she had for collateral was her old car. A loan from her mom? That might work.

She stood up and walked over to the side table by a chair she supposed was meant to be inviting, but the thing looked as comfortable as a brick. She picked up the note.

Piper,

You were finally sleeping, so I didn't wake you. I've gone to make arrangements to take Topher home. There's yogurt, fruit, cereal, and milk in the refrigerator. Please don't leave the room before I return. I'll be back by noon.

B.

THANK GOD. She drew a shaky breath. She could pay back Bear for any cost. It might take her some time, but he'd understand. At least, she thought he would. Piper let the paper drop and leaned back in the chair. Don't leave. Right. Where would she go? She knew no one in Washington. She glanced at the clock and did a double take. It was almost noon. Her gaze moved down to the T-shirt she was wearing. It hung to her thighs. She needed to change.

She moved, not because she wanted to but because she had to. A lethargy surrounded her like a shroud. Her body ached, which made sense since her heart had been torn out of her chest last night. Christopher, her big brother and hero, was dead.

In her mind's eye, she saw him on that table. What had happened?

Piper swiped at the tears that fell. She didn't even try to stop them. She pulled clothes out of her bag and moved into the bathroom, where she stopped in front of the mirror. Her eyes were puffy and swollen, and her face was blotched with red. Her hair was riotous from going to bed with it wet, but she didn't care. Piper dressed, brushed her teeth, and pulled her hair to the top of her head. She wrapped a strand of hair around the bun she'd made and tucked it underneath itself. It would hold.

She dropped back into the chair and lifted her feet onto the furniture, grasping her legs and linking her fingers so she could put her chin on her knees. She stared at the courier bag. *Why? Why was it so important to you, Christopher?*

Piper unfolded and retrieved the pouch, then opened the bag and pulled out the first book. She reverently opened the cover. "If it was important to you, we'll find it."

She leaned back and started to read. She had to be missing something. Her eyes pulled back to the depictions of the stamps that Christopher had meticulously recreated in his notes. "What are you trying to tell me?"

She turned the page as a series of thuds sounded in the hallway, disregarding the noise. A maid with a cart or perhaps a wheeled suitcase …

A loud thud followed two loud bangs. Piper knew what those sounds were. *Gunshots*. She grabbed her brother's notebooks and bag and ran into the bathroom. After slamming the door shut, she locked the deadbolt as someone pounded on the door to the room. Piper scrambled for her phone. She had to call Bear.

The banging got louder. Piper scrolled to her outgoing calls. She hit send as soon as she found his number. She got inside the bathtub, moving away from the bathroom door.

"Hey, I'm almost there," Bear said when he picked up.

"Someone's trying to break in!" She jumped when a loud thud sounded against the door. "I'm coming. Get in the bathroom and lock the door."

"I have. Hurry, God. Please hurry!"

She sank to her knees in the tub and waited. "They stopped."

"Piper, don't leave the bathroom. Stay there until I get there."

"I'm—" She screamed when she heard another gunshot.

"I'm outside. I'm coming in!" Bear yelled. Piper sat down and wrapped her arm around her legs, shivering. She held the phone to her ear and rocked back and forth. More shouting, thuds, and another gunshot—so many loud noises. Then after the sounds had stilled, she heard sirens. Piper turned and looked at the bathroom door. No, she wouldn't move. She would stay there until Bear came to get her because he would come. He promised he'd protect her.

CHAPTER 12

Bear slammed down on the brakes, and threw the SUV into Park behind a row of cars in the hotel's parking lot. He sprinted through the front of the hotel and disregarded the staff as they tried to warn him not to go down the hall. He rounded the corner at a full-out run.

His mind shifted as he assessed the situation. Colten was down, and three men were at the door of his room. One was rearing back to kick the door as Bear flew into them. He fell among the other men but was on his feet before the others knew they'd been dropped.

His opponents didn't have defenses up, and his training in martial arts taught him to take advantage of those gaps. Bear dropped to his knee and struck the closest man using a throat punch. As the second man reached for his weapon, Bear jumped to both feet and struck the wrist that held the gun with his foot. The snap of his leg propelled the gun in the other direction, and it fired. With his weight still on his back foot, Bear struck with his foot again, snapping the man's head back. The body went limp, and Bear made his way to the third man. The bastard sprung to his knees and slashed wildly with a knife in one hand. A gun was in the other, but it was empty, the receiver locked to the rear.

Bear took a step back and waited for the man to lunge with the knife again. In the fraction of a second it took for the man to move, Bear had lined his body in position, and with his right foot forward, he jumped, forcing himself past his opponent's guard. Bear timed the kick with the fall of his body. With his left leg extended, Bear flew forward into the man's chest, forcing him backward. The knife and gun clenched in his hands were the endpoints of useless arms flailing toward Bear from his kick's force.

The man dropped to the floor, and his head bounced on the hard tile. The resounding thud of his skull told Bear his opponent wouldn't get up again. Ever.

He raced over to Colten and turned the man over. Blood coated his chest. "Fuck."

Reaching into his pocket, pulled out his phone and disconnected the call to Piper before hitting dial.

"Operator—"

"This is McGowen. I have a Guardian down at my location. Gunshot." He put the phone down and whipped off his t-shirt, wadding it up and holding it against the wound in Colten's chest. "Medical ASAP." He also shouted the name of the hotel he was staying at in case she didn't know.

Bear heard the sirens. He held the pressure on the wound and looked back at the fuckers he'd taken down. One was dead. A second was dying. The third man, the one he'd punched in the throat, was choking because Bear had shattered his trachea. He didn't give a flying fuck.

"Police!"

Bear didn't move. "Guardian. I need EMT here, now!" He turned his head to see the police advancing toward him with guns drawn and aimed at him. "My shield is in my back pocket," Bear said, not moving so he could keep the pressure on Colten's wound.

He felt his creds being removed. "Turn your face to me," one of the officers said.

Bear looked at the cop. "Guardian security is on that phone." He nodded to his cell phone.

"What the fuck happened?" His creds were dropped beside him.

"They went after the person in the room. Medical?"

"They're pulling up now," a different cop said as they moved down to the three men. "What the hell happened to them?"

I did, Bear thought, but he was smart enough not to say a fucking word. When the EMT relieved him, Bear sat back on his heels and grabbed his phone. He lifted and put the phone to his ear. "There were supposed to be two Guardians stationed here. Can you contact the second one?"

"Hold, please." The operator's voice remained as calm as ever. Fuck. He glanced down as the EMTs worked on Colten.

"There's no answer. Her last reported position was the rear of the building."

Bear walked down to the cops who were

standing by the dead men. "There was supposed to be another Guardian at the rear of the building."

"Roger." The sergeant on the scene repeated the information on his radio. Thirty seconds later, the radio squawked again. "One female down at the rear of the hotel."

The sergeant lifted his eyes to Bear. "We'll need you to come with us."

"That's not happening." A police officer walked down the hall. Lieutenant bars sparkled on his collar. "Sir, are you Bear McGowen?"

"I am."

"I'll escort you and the person you're protecting to your transportation."

"But, sir," the sergeant waved at the dead men. "We have three dead men."

"Very good, Clooney, you can count. I'm following orders from people way above us."

"Sir, the press is outside."

"Fuck, front or back?"

"Front."

"Have someone pull my vehicle around to the rear without making a show about it. Sir, instead of escorting you, I'll be driving you."

Bear nodded and watched as Colten was transferred to a stretcher. "I need to go get her. Give me some time to settle her down."

"I'll be right here," the lieutenant said, walking over to where his men had retreated.

Bear picked up his credentials, pulled out the keycard to the room, and went to the door. He swiped the card. Nothing. He swiped it again. Nothing. No lights at all. No red or green signals.

Rearing back, he kicked the door, and it slammed in. "Piper, it's okay. It's me," he called out as he entered the room. "Piper?" He tried the handle to the bathroom.

The lock was released, and Piper threw herself into his arms. "I don't want to stay here any longer." She pulled away and gasped. "Blood. Are you hurt?"

Bear looked down at his arms and hands. "No, Colten, who was outside, was shot. We've got to move."

Piper gripped her courier bag, and he could read the stress in her expression. "They'll find me again."

He moved to cup her neck, but the blood on his hands stopped him. "Get your things, and would you bring me a shirt."

"Where's yours?"

"I used it to stem the flow of blood." He grabbed the tiny ass bar of soap in the bathroom and scrubbed.

"Here." She put a button-down shirt on the vanity and dipped back out of the bathroom.

"No, they won't find you. Not this time. Not where we're going." He had no idea where that was, but completely off-grid was what they'd said at the meeting.

"I wasn't even registered here," she said. He could hear her moving around in the room.

"I was. I went to the morgue with you and signed us both in." Which was a rookie fucking mistake. *But who in the hell had access to the sign-in logs at the morgue?*

She came back to the doorway as he toweled off. "Who has access to the sign-in logs?"

"Exactly what I just asked myself." He shoved his arms through the shirt and quickly buttoned it. He took all the bags, including the courier bag, from her and grasped them in one hand as they walked toward the door. "I want you to do me a favor."

She stopped and looked up at him. Her eyes were huge and luminous compared to the pallor of her face. "Anything."

"Close your eyes, and let me guide you out of the door. I'll let you know when you can open them."

"Is it that bad?" She was shaking so hard that her teeth were chattering.

He took her hand and placed it against his chest. "Trust me, Piper, please. Close your eyes. I'll lead you where you need to go; nothing will hurt you. I promise."

She stared at him. "You've never lied to me."

"No, I haven't." He locked his gaze with her. "And I never will."

She nodded. "I trust you." She closed her eyes, and he led her by the hand out the door. The cops were working the scene. Evidence markers littered the hallway, and bullet holes were marked. The dead men were exactly as they'd fallen.

Contrary to popular belief, cops didn't move dead bodies and couldn't gather evidence until the coroner released the scene. Bear had learned that on one of his many missions for Guardian, so he knew the bodies would still be in the hall. He maneuvered around the dead men and walked her down the hall.

"Can I open my eyes?" she asked as they continued walking.

"Not yet." He wasn't sure if the female Guardian was alive or dead. When he made it to the door, he looked outside. There was no ambulance and nobody waiting for a coroner. Bear glanced around the corner of the building. There. An ambulance, evidence markers, and tape around bushes. He hoped the Guardian was okay. The lieutenant stood by his car. "You can open your eyes now."

Piper did, but she didn't let go of his hand. He opened the door. "The lieutenant will give us a ride."

"But what about the SUV?" Piper asked as he opened the back door for her.

"Guardian can pick it up later." He shut her in, then went to the other side and got in.

"The press had to have been listening to us via scanner. I have no other idea how they got here so fast," the lieutenant said as he started the vehicle and drove out of the parking lot by going over a curb and into another hotel's parking area.

Bear grabbed Piper's hand again, only to feel her shaking like a leaf. He reached into her courier bag, pulled out her prescription, and offered her one.

"No, two," she said and looked up at him. "Trust me. I need it."

He shook out another pill, and she swallowed both without water. "Where are we going?"

The lieutenant answered, "A private airport."

Bear lifted his arm, and Piper scooted over. He dropped his arm around her and held her. As he watched the city go by out the window, he wondered where in the hell Guardian could hide Piper. Another giant question remained and hopefully would solve whatever the hell was going on. What was in that damn notebook?

CHAPTER 13

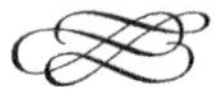

Piper walked up the stairs of the little black jet. Little compared to the plane they flew to Washington in, but it was spacious and luxurious. She sat down and buckled her seatbelt, although no one told her to do so. Bear went to the back of the plane and came back with a small bottle of water.

She drank it and thanked him. Doubling her pills had the desired effect. She was numb. And being numb right then was a good thing. If she hadn't taken two, it would have been only a matter of time before she was curled into a fetal position and crippled by anxiety.

The man she assumed was the pilot smiled at her when he exited the cockpit. He pulled up the steps and closed the door. Once finished, he turned to them. "Flight time is about two hours. Once we get to cruising altitude, you're free to move about. If you're seated, please keep your seat-belts on. The galley is fully stocked. We ask that you clip the cabinets shut after you open them. I'll announce when we're cleared for takeoff and when we start our descent. Enjoy the ride."

Bear sat down beside her and took her hand. "How do you feel?"

She turned to look at him. "Numb."

"So, no need to hold your hand while we take off?"

She blinked and then tried to muster a smile. "I think you should, just in case."

His thumb stroked the back of her hand. "I think I should, too."

The feel of his touch quelled a bit of the noise lingering just past the drug-induced numbness. The taxi and takeoff seemed to take only a few minutes. Nothing like the wait for clearance on the trip there. She glanced down at her hand in Bear's. His thumb continued to rub back and forth over the back of her hand. "I'm not weak," she said, looking at him. "I'm not. I know you've only seen my issues, but I'm not weak."

"I don't think you're weak." He turned to her. "You kept it together today without medication."

"I took two pills." She snorted.

"*After* the incident. After the gunshots and the fact that someone was trying to get into the room. After you called me. After you packed us up. After you got me a shirt. After you trusted me to get you out of the building by closing your eyes. You made it through the worst of the situation."

She considered that for a moment. She'd been terrified, but an attack hadn't crippled her. "It was only a matter of time." Dismissing his words with the certainty of her past, she'd been in the cycle so often she knew she'd have one if she hadn't medicated. And that was another reason for her panic attacks, according to her doctor. The fear of having one also raised her anxiety. She was a mess.

"Guardian is taking Topher back to Baton Rouge. They want to know if there's someplace you want him interred."

Piper sighed and closed her eyes. "He has a place already. By his mom." She told him the name of the cemetery. Christopher had taken her to his mom's gravesite, and she'd been shocked to see a stone with his name on it. His birth date was filled in, but not his date of death. *He'd laughed at her. "Everyone dies, Piper. There's no escaping it."*

Bear continued to hold her hand. "I'll let them know. He also had three life insurance policies. A million dollars each."

Even through the comforting feeling of numbness, she jerked her head around. "What?"

"You're the beneficiary. You'll be able to afford to continue your studies without teaching."

She slowly returned her gaze to the front of the cabin. "I'm not sure I'll do that."

"Which? Continue your studies or work?" Bear asked.

"Continue my education. The idea of working with Christopher is what kept me in the program. I was close to dropping out when I met him. I love the idea of teaching, but I can do that without a doctoral degree."

"What would you teach?"

"Well, physics." She rolled her eyes, and he laughed.

"Perhaps I should rephrase that. What grade level would you teach?"

She considered that for a moment. "Not high school. I barely survived it once. I couldn't imagine living it day after day." She'd loved track and school, taking every advanced placement course she could take. She wasn't in the "in" crowd and had only two friends who were semi-close. She wasn't invited to prom or any of the dances. Her father told her the term wallflower was coined to describe her. He made fun of her when she'd cried about not being asked to a dance at school. She'd learned not to show emotion. Her dad would belittle her or tease her mercilessly. Another reason for her anxiety, according to her doctor.

When she moved to the dorm at the university, boys started to notice her. They asked her out, and some became friends. Most pursued sex, which was why her experience with men had come in college.

"College, then. Could you do that without a doctorate?"

She blinked and grasped for what they'd been talking about. "Oh, yes. The minimum requirement is a master's degree. Some colleges require more, but college professors are accepted with master's degree."

"Any college in particular?"

She shook her head. "Wherever I can find a position."

He nodded. “Good to know. Did you eat breakfast?”

She shook her head.

“Let’s go back to the galley and see what they have.” Bear took off his seatbelt and extended his hand to her.

She unbuckled her belt and took his hand. When they found the galley, Piper sat down at a table permanently affixed to the floor. The chairs were, too, but the seats swiveled, and she could sit down easily enough. There was also a seatbelt, which she fastened.

She watched as Bear explored the cabinets, pulling bread, sandwich meats, cheeses, mayo, and mustard out of the various compartments. She watched as he made two sandwiches, grabbed two small bags of chips, and brought them to the table. He put one portion in front of her, but she had no desire to eat.

“I’m not hungry.” She should be, but she wasn’t.

“I know, but you should eat anyway.” Bear sat down and buckled up. He opened her chips and poured them out onto the plate.

She picked one up and broke it in half before putting it in her mouth. Then she worked on the sandwich and was able to eat about a quarter.

Instead of eating, she focused on the plate and looked at its continuing square patterns. She traced it with her fingernail and looked over at Bear. "The answer has to be in those stamps."

Bear stopped with a chip halfway to his mouth. "Gut feeling?"

She nodded. "He must have noticed something and went to Dr. Franklin to verify what he saw."

"Or question him," Bear suggested. "When we get to where we're going, Guardian wants the notebooks photocopied so they can be digitized. They believe that with your transcribed notes, they can build a key and transcribe his notes faster than you could."

"That makes sense." She traced the square on her plate again. "When did Christopher die?"

Bear looked at her. "I don't know, why?"

She looked at him. "Because if it was the day he went to see Dr. Franklin, that would be a big coincidence, wouldn't it?"

Bear nodded. "A big coincidence."

She stared down at the plate and placed her finger on one side of it and one finger on the other side of the geometric design. "In physics, there's a *cause* and a *result*." She lifted a finger and replaced it when she said cause and then did the same when she said result. It was what she'd been missing in his notes. She'd been reading it as a journal, not as his notes. He wasn't leaving a narrative. He was leaving his work. Piper looked up at Bear, who was watching her intently. "There are no coincidences." She pointed at the square on her plate. "The cause ... and then the result. Even if it *wasn't* what you anticipated, it is a result. We need to study both." Piper tapped the plate with her fingernail. "The request was the cause. The processed report was the result." She gasped. "The cause and result have to be included in the process they used to give him the reports."

Bear stared at her. "I have no idea what that process is."

"Neither do I, but we need to find out. It has to be why he highlighted each of those stamps. Why he recreated them so meticulously."

"Then we have a way forward."

Bear gazed out the window as they landed. The mountains were impressive, as was the pilot's skill at landing them in the valley. The touchdown was smooth, and the engine reversed immediately, telling him the runway was short. He'd made enough combat landings to know by how quickly the engines reversed that the landing strip was small. They turned at the end of the runway and taxied back. The plane rolled to a stop, and the engine noise disappeared. The pilot appeared and headed to the doorway. He opened it and then hit the hydraulics to lower the steps. Bear unfastened his seatbelt and stood up. Piper was beside him before he could stretch. He grabbed her hand and took the courier bag from her, slinging it over his shoulder. They exited the plane, and Bear glanced around. An old truck sat by the side of the runway.

"Is that our ride?" Piper asked.

"I believe it is." Bear thanked the pilot and took their bags in his free hand before they made their way over to the truck. A smile tugged on his lips when he saw who was waiting for them. "I never thought I'd see you again. I thought you'd be living in China." Or buried there, which was the more logical ending to that mission.

The man he knew as Bengal walked out to greet him. Bengal pulled him into a bro hug before grabbing Bear by the shoulders. "You were on the team I traveled with for a while." He narrowed his eyes. "Bear, right?"

"That's right, and you're—"

Just as he was about to say Bengal, the man interrupted, "Zane. Zane Reynolds. That was one heck of a mission. Ended up lasting about six months for me."

"Our part wasn't too difficult. I know you had the difficult end." It was a mission he'd been on while in the military. God, almost a lifetime ago. He took Piper's hand again. "This is Piper Whitehead."

Zane smiled. "Hi. My wife and I are looking forward to a bit of company. We love the seclusion, but having someone to visit with now and then is a good thing."

Zane took the bags from him, and they moved toward the truck. "Has Guardian stopped paying?" Bear chuckled.

"Ah, this truck looks like it's on its last legs, but under the hood, it's all new, all power, and yet it still fits in with the neighborhood, if you get my drift." Zane got in and turned on the ignition. Bear opened the passenger side door, and Piper hesitated. Sitting on the bench seat, she'd sit next to Ben … ah, Zane.

He settled her dilemma and got in first. The look of relief was instantaneous. Thankfully, Zane didn't say a word about the oddness of him being in the middle. The guy got points for that. After Piper got in and shut the door, they started moving, bouncing down the pitted roadway and coming out on a paved road. Once they'd stopped bouncing and cruised down the highway, Zane chuckled. "I do have to warn you that we have a new household member, so things could get a little crazy."

Piper leaned forward to see him. "A baby?"

"Yes, definitely. Dude is a huge baby, but he's more of an Irish Wolfhound mixed with Timber-wolf type of baby. He's a handful, but he's friendly … for the most part. He didn't appreciate a skunk getting too close to my wife last week. Needless to say, it was a stinky situation for some time. I had to drive to the city to get the chemical wash to de-skunkify both the pup and my wife."

Bear heard Piper's musical laughter for the first time. Her smile was wide, and she looked younger and absolutely beautiful. Her eyes danced as she shook her head. "I had a golden retriever growing up. Daisy found out the hard way that skunks were not to be messed with." She shook her head and sighed. "She had to sleep outside in the doghouse for two weeks."

"I didn't have that option. My wife wouldn't have liked sleeping outside."

Piper laughed again, and Bear smiled widely. He'd pay to hear that laugh again. They drove up a winding mountain road. The trees hung over the road, precariously in some locations, roots gripping massive rocks and boulders. There were hairpin curves that made Bear uncomfortable, but Zane kept the speed constant and drove as if he was the only person on the road. Zane pulled under a rock overhang beside two other vehicles. A fancy SUV and a dual-axled truck. Beside the truck, there was a trailer. "This is the garage. We have a bit of a hike to get to the house."

Piper gave Bear a curious look, and he shrugged. When they got out of the truck, Zane took one bag, and Bear took another. Taking Piper's hand, Bear followed Zane up a winding trail.

"Where's the house?" Piper whispered to him when he let her go in front of him when the trail narrowed.

Zane chuckled. "Not too far now."

The trail leveled out, and Zane took a hard right. They walked along a rock wall, and that was when Bear saw it. "You live inside the mountain?"

Zane turned around and winked. "Pretty cool, huh?"

Piper stopped and looked at the entrance. "Cool is an understatement."

"Wow, when Guardian says off-grid, they mean it." Bear held Piper's hand as they approached the door. It slid open, and Zane dropped the bag to catch the dog that leaped at him. The dog wiggled wildly, yipping, licking, and squirming as he mauled his owner. Zane's laughter rang down the mountainside. As he put the dog down, the puppy realized other people were with his master. The dog took aim at Piper and bounded toward them. Bear caught the dog in mid-air before he flattened Piper. He'd never been bathed in dog slime before. He hoped he'd never have another one. But the sheer joy and happiness of the wiggling dog in his arms made up for the immediate need for a shower.

"Sorry! I'm so sorry," a tall woman with long black hair said as she pulled the dog off him. "Dude, that isn't cool."

Zane grabbed the dog by the collar and made him sit. The animal's tail wagged a mile a minute. "I've got him if you want to introduce yourself." Zane was talking to Piper.

She inched forward with her palm extended. The dog sniffed her and then started licking her hand. "Hi, Dude." The puppy jumped a bit, but Piper didn't seem to mind. Sitting as he was, his head was almost as high as Piper's chest.

"How old is he?" Bear asked as he used his shirt sleeve to wipe the doggy drool off his cheek.

"Five months," the woman said. "Hi, I'm Jewell."

"My wife," Zane said from where he held the dog. "Babe, this is Bear and Piper. I met Bear before I started working with you."

"Oh, that's cool. Nice to meet you," Jewell said and turned to Piper. "I'm sorry if he scared you."

"No, I adore animals." Piper smiled at the other woman. "He's a lover, isn't he?" Piper had both hands on the dog, scratching his scruff.

"As long as you aren't a skunk." Jewell snorted.

Piper laughed. "We heard about that."

Jewell rolled her eyes. "*Everyone* has heard about that. I will never live it down. My brothers and sisters are insane. I now have a skunk collection. I've been receiving little gifts from everyone in my family. Nephews and nieces included."

"Babe, how about you take our guests in and settle them, and I'll take Dude for a quick run."

"Okay. I ran three miles with him this morning

after you left. He slept for a half hour and then was ready to go again." Jewell turned back to the automatic door. "This way." She walked in the door, and Piper followed. Bear grabbed the bag Zane had dropped and followed the ladies as Zane and the dog headed down the mountain.

"Wow." Bear stopped at the top of a long ramp. The door shut behind him. In front of him was a vast cave. He could see how the cave had been sectioned from where he was. A kitchen area and a storage area were to the left. To the right, a massive fireplace and a sectional that could probably accommodate an entire football team. A large television was in the corner of the room. He walked down the ramp to where Jewell was showing Piper the kitchen.

"This is our pride and joy. A pizza oven." She grinned. "I told Zane we needed one when we moved up here. I love pizza. Of course, he's found ways to make it healthy, but he's a great cook." After a compliment from Piper, Jewell turned and walked up a different rock ramp angled in another direction. "I'll show you to your room," Jewell said.

At the top, they turned left. "This is my office. I'm afraid it's a classified area, and neither of you has adequate clearance to go in there, so Zane and

I changed the small bedroom into an office for you. Sorry for the hodgepodge of desk and chairs, but hopefully, it'll suit your needs." She opened a door. A table had been set up with two office chairs on either side and a computer on top. "I have a scanner for you, too. Con said you'd need one to send him copies of a notebook. I'll hook that up for you after dinner."

Jewell continued to the next room. "Here's your room." She opened the door. A queen-sized bed filled the room. "Through there is your bathroom. All our lights are on sensors. The shower is, too. The water is always warm, so you don't need to worry about running it before you get in. Our room is down at the end of the hall. I'll let you get settled. I have to check in and make sure the world hasn't fallen apart. Zane will call us when it's time to eat. Make yourself at home, and I'm sorry about Dude."

Piper's eyes were wide, but Bear thanked Jewell and entered the room. After a goodbye, the woman headed back to her office.

Piper stood by the door. "Only one bed."

Bear put down the bags on the floor. "I can sleep on the couch downstairs. There's plenty of room."

Piper wrapped her arms around herself, looked up at the rock ceiling, and then back to the dark passage to what Bear believed was the bathroom. "I don't want to stay here alone."

Bear sat down on the bed and extended a hand to Piper. "I can sleep on top of the covers like I did at the hotel."

Piper took his hand and walked up to him. "I'm sorry." She shook her head.

"For what?"

"You always have to accommodate me." She bit her bottom lip. "You must be tired of my baggage."

Bear put his finger under her chin. "Not in the slightest." Bear examined her face. She was exhausted. Probably both mentally and physically. Grief could affect the body with a physical force. "Let's get our stuff put away and then go for a walk outside."

She shook her head. "We need to find the reason Christopher was killed."

"And we will. But to do that, you and I need to be able to concentrate. A walk, dinner, sleep, and in the morning, with fresh minds, we can make better strides than examining the problem when we're exhausted."

She closed her eyes and filled her lungs with air. "I am tired."

"We both are." He hadn't slept much the night before, and the adrenaline rush of the day had left its mark. "If you're uncomfortable with me being in here with you, just say the word, and Dude and I will share his bed. It's probably big enough to stretch out on."

"Dude wouldn't let you sleep." She smiled a bit. "I'm not uncomfortable."

He smiled and kissed the back of her hand. "Neither am I. I'll wash off Dude's slobber, and then we'll go for a walk. Why don't you change into some workout clothes? I need some exercise. Sound good?"

Her eyes were on their hands. She lifted her gaze and smiled. "That sounds wonderful."

CHAPTER 14

Piper stood under the showerhead. Her body was tired from the "walk." They'd gone straight down the mountain at a jog and then sprinted back up when the trail allowed them. She needed the workout more than she realized. Focused on the terrain, she didn't have time to think about Christopher or dwell on that damned stamp. She'd had to watch every footfall placement and monitor her next jump, where the rocks jutted out, or how to propel herself up after Bear.

She'd trailed after him, and Lord, the man was phenomenal. His strength and grace as he moved from one ledge to another, then sprinted forward, was beautiful to watch. He moved with the grace of someone who knew exactly what he could do. He'd turn and give her a hand up at times. She'd take his help, especially when the jump was almost as long as she was tall. He'd extended back and grasped her hand while hanging onto a tree. When she'd jumped, he'd pulled, and she'd landed against his chest. His arm belted around her until she had her feet under her.

Piper had looked up at him and drew a breath. He'd dropped his head down and kissed her lips before releasing her and sprinting thirty feet up the mountain. She didn't have time to overthink that kiss, then, but she was making up for lost time. What was the purpose of the kiss? Did he mean to do it? *Well, duh, Piper, he kissed you. He didn't fall over and land on you, and your lips collided by accident. Idiot.*

She dropped her head back and groaned. *Okay, so he kissed you. So, what?*

So, what? She reached for the shampoo and used a palmful to lather her hair. It was probably nothing to him. He was so handsome that he probably had plenty of sex. *A kiss to him wouldn't mean anything.*

But it meant something to her. She dropped her head back to rinse out the suds. It meant … she cocked her head under the water, then moved forward out of the shower and opened her eyes. She had a crush on the man, didn't she?

Piper sighed. "Of course, you do." She poured some conditioner into her hand and worked it through the knotted mess her hair had turned into throughout the day. Well, as long as she was aware of it, she'd take steps to ensure she didn't embarrass herself. The probability of anything between them developing was infinitesimal. She was pretty sure she wasn't his type. She could see him with a tall blonde on his arm. Some supermodel type. The ones she'd seen on social media with beautiful white smiles and perfect bodies.

Piper lifted onto her toes and then dropped back down. She was short. Five feet two inches. *Almost.* She wore a size two and sometimes shopped in the girl's section of the stores when she was looking for clothes. She was a B cup and had mousey brown hair. Her mouth was too big for her face. She sighed. She was in shape because she loved to run. It was her outlet. No, she wasn't the type of person Bear would fall for. The kiss had to be just a … fluke.

She leaned back and washed out the hair conditioner. A fluke. Yes, an anomaly. She settled that thought and locked it into place before she turned off the water. After toweling off and getting dressed, she walked back into the bedroom. Bear was going to shower downstairs in the gym. Zane had shown him where that was, and she was surprised they'd have a gym when they had the outdoors, but Zane explained that during the winter, there wasn't much of an opportunity to be outside. She hadn't thought about being in the cave during the winter. It would be lovely as long as there was heat and food.

Piper braided her wet hair and let the braid fall down her back. Then she dressed in jeans and the Witness Protection t-shirt Honor had insisted she take. When she opened the door, Dude was sitting outside. His tail wagged faster than a fan set to max speed, so she stopped and loved on him for a minute. When they walked down the ramp, it was together, and the dog's haunches were as high as her hips. He was going to be massive when he finished growing and filled out.

Piper heard voices in the kitchen, and she and Dude walked toward that section of the cave. "Hey, Bear said you guys had a good workout," Jewell greeted her when she entered.

"It was fantastic." She accepted a bottle of water

from Zane. "Thank you." She opened it and downed half of it. "I'm usually a flat road runner. I think I'll be sore in the morning."

"It takes some getting used to, but if you want to run the roads, just follow the trail to the garage. You can run down the road we came up. I have cameras and alarms on it from the bottom up. No one comes up here without permission, so you can run without worries of vehicles." Zane emptied a large pan of pasta into a strainer.

"That sounds like a plan. Can I help with anything?" Piper looked around for Bear but didn't see him.

"No, we've got this," Jewell said.

"Bear's in the gym. Would you mind telling him that dinner will be ready in five minutes?" Zane asked.

"Where is it?" She turned around to look at the cave.

"Through the living room. It used to be a hydroponics garden, but neither of us has a green thumb, so we remodeled."

Jewell snorted. "If I could grow chocolate bars, we'd still have it."

Zane leaned over. "You can't." He kissed her, and she laughed.

Piper ducked out of the kitchen, not wanting to be the third wheel. Dude followed her through the kitchen and into the gym, where she stopped in the doorway and watched as Bear moved. His arms and legs followed a certain pattern. Almost as if he was practicing the moves. He noticed her and stopped. "Hey, this is pretty cool, isn't it?" He expanded his arms and turned in a circle. She saw the thick blue pad he was on, and a treadmill, a stationary bike, an elliptical, and one side was nothing but free weights.

"It's bigger than the gym in my neighborhood." Which was true. They had so much equipment crammed into such a small space that she had gone to the gym once and never went back. The lack of personal space was a huge no-go for her. "What were you doing?"

"I was running through my kata while waiting for you."

"What's that?"

"In the martial arts, specifically the Japanese forms, a kata is a practice. The word actually means form. It's a method of perfecting your form and posture."

"It looked choreographed." She cocked her head at him as he walked up to her.

"It is one hundred percent choreographed and meant to be practiced. It's the third discipline I've learned. So, it's still relatively new to me, and I practice the kata as much as possible." He pointed at her shirt. "I see Honor got you to take it."

She pulled the shirt out and looked down. "She didn't give me a choice. What type of martial arts is that?" She nodded to where he'd been.

"Goju-ryu. I decided to study it because it has a strong focus on breathing and is designed to develop a harmony between one's brain and body."

Piper looked back at the matt. "Would I have to fight to learn how to do that?"

Bear glanced at her and then back at the mat. "No. The kata is a singular lesson of movements and form. The movements can be taught without learning how to fight. Would you like to learn?"

Piper glanced around the gym. "I think I would. I should probably learn how to do some self-defense, too. But that's just not me."

Bear took both of her hands in his. "I can show you self-defense moves." He started walking backward toward the thick blue mat on the floor.

"Jewell and Zane said dinner would be ready in five minutes." She wasn't sold on the idea of learning any moves.

He lifted his eyebrows and smiled. "Five minutes?"

"Less than that now." She shook her head. "I don't think I can learn anything in that time."

Bear stopped walking but pulled her to him and stared down at her. "You realize I kissed you today?"

She blinked at the left turn the conversation made. "I do. It was a fluke." She dipped her chin in a nod, agreeing with herself.

"A fluke." Bear shook his head. "It most certainly wasn't a fluke. I'd been looking for an opportunity to do that."

"What? Why?"

He pulled her into him. "Because I wanted to kiss you." He bent down, and his lips drifted over hers in a soft touch. "If you don't want this, tell me to stop."

Stop? No, she wouldn't tell him to stop. She hoped he'd never stop and God, she hoped he wasn't just playing with her. No, that wasn't who he was. She hadn't known him long, but she knew him better than she knew anyone else in the world. She sighed and toed up, touching her lips against his. His hand slid up her back to the nape of her neck. He licked her lips, and she opened for him.

He didn't force himself on her but led the dance of their tongues. When he broke the kiss, he smiled down at her. "Not a fluke."

She shook her head. "I guess not." She felt a nudge at her hip and looked down. Dude was there, his nose pushing between them.

Bear laughed, loosened his grip on her, and reached down to give Dude some attention. "He's not bad when he's tuckered out." Bear chuckled when the dog's tongue lolled out. His tail swished as rapidly as it had when he met Piper at the bedroom door.

"We should go eat," Bear said as he took her hand and led her out of the gym. The lights in the living room turned on as they walked through the massive area. Piper's mind reeled. *Because he wanted to ... how long would he be interested? Why was that important? Because she didn't want to have her heart that had just been shattered into a million pieces trampled on. She'd never recover. She needed to know what his intentions were.* She needed to ask him that.

"There you are," Jewell said happily as she opened a wine bottle. "Pasta carbonara, salad, garlic bread, and wine." She poured a small portion into each glass.

Bear pulled out her chair for Piper, and she slid

into it. The food looked amazing, and she was hungry for the first time in days, probably because of the workout.

She watched as Jewell ate what her husband had put on her plate. She thought it was strange that he was serving her, but she took her pasta as the bowl passed. She ate the salad first, without dressing. Christopher thought she was insane for not using dressing. She blinked and looked down. Christopher. A wave of remorse bashed against her. Here she was, lost in her thoughts about a kiss and enjoying dinner, and Christopher would never have the opportunity to do either.

"Would you like something else?" Zane asked her.

She blinked and looked up at him. "I'm sorry, what?"

"The food, would you like something else?" He pointed to her untouched food.

"Oh, no, thank you." She glanced at Bear, and he put his hand on her thigh under the table.

"Piper lost her brother, and we're working the case to find out why he was murdered. It is still hard to internalize."

"Oh, man. I knew that." Jewell sighed and slouched back in her chair. "I didn't tell you, Zane.

I got sidetracked. I'm so sorry." She looked from Zane to her. "I can't imagine how you feel right now."

Piper tried to smile. "The emotion just hits me hard sometimes." Like a bomb exploding directly in front of her.

"I can only imagine," Zane acknowledged. "We put the scanner in the small room. If you need anything tomorrow, knock on our office door, and I'll get you what you need."

"That's fine, thank you," Bear replied for them. "Tonight, we're going to sleep and then try to slay that dragon in the morning."

Piper made an effort to eat her food. Bear emptied his wine and put his empty glass in front of her, taking her portion and placing it in front of himself. She swiveled her head to look at him. "You don't drink." He lifted his eyebrows a couple of times. "I do."

She rolled her eyes and took another bite of the pasta. "This is very good, thank you."

"You're welcome. Tomorrow, we'll do pizza." Jewell seemed to almost levitate off her chair. "Zane also makes a delicious desert pizza."

Piper was curious. "How do you do that?"

"Pizza crust with pie filling smeared on top of

it. When it comes out of the oven, sprinkle it with confectioner's sugar."

Jewell reached over and put her hand on Piper's. "Absolutely amazing."

"I think you give me too much credit." Zane chuckled and finished the last of his wine.

"No, I don't give you enough credit," Jewell shot the reply back at him. "I was living off energy drinks and pizza when we met. If Zane hadn't changed my diet, I'd be four hundred pounds and living with coronary heart disease."

"You haven't gained or lost a pound since I met you." Zane offered his wife some more wine, which she accepted.

"Bear?" Zane asked.

"No, thank you, I'm drinking Piper's. She doesn't drink."

Jewell laughed. "I don't know if we can be friends now."

Piper smiled. "I never developed a taste for it."

"Oh, I know someone like that. She said she tried every cocktail you could imagine but never found anything she liked. Then she tried cold red wine. Says she loves it." Jewell shrugged. "I can't imagine drinking cold red wine, but hey, whatever trips your trigger, right?"

"I guess," Piper answered. She wasn't going to try any other types of alcohol. She'd seen how stupid people in college got when they drank it and couldn't imagine losing control and being miserable the next day with dehydration, headache, and nausea. Not her idea of a good time. She heard a soft whine and turned around. Dude was waiting patiently at the doorway of the kitchen.

"That's my cue." Zane stood up. "Come on, boy. Let's go for our nightly outing."

The dog danced in the doorway, obviously trained not to enter the kitchen. "Can I help with dishes?" Piper asked as Jewell started to remove the plates from the table.

"No, not tonight. You guys must be exhausted. I'll take you up on the offer tomorrow, but tonight, you're guests. Tomorrow, you're family and can help with the dishes." Jewell laughed and waved them out of the kitchen. "Go on. I'll get this."

"Are you ready to go to sleep?" Bear asked her as they walked out of the kitchen.

"Not really."

"Then let's go outside and look at the stars. They must be spectacular here." Bear walked with her up the large ramp and out of the cave. They walked hand in hand, the moonlight more than adequate to see. Zane was below them, playing with Dude. He tossed a stick, and the dog chased after it.

"Look at that." Bear pointed toward the sky, and she gasped at the multitude of stars she could see. "That's beautiful. There are so many."

"No light pollution to block your view." Bear climbed onto a large rock and turned around, offering her a hand. He pulled her up after him, and they sat down. She searched the heavens for a while. "Why did you want to kiss me?" She turned to him. "No riddles, please. I'm trying hard to process why you'd want to kiss me, and I'm coming up empty. Maybe the real question is, what is this leading to?"

"I think you're attractive, sexy actually, and I like you." Bear shrugged as if that was the easiest answer in the world to come up with. "I'm not sure where it will lead."

That wasn't an answer. Well, it was, but not the one she wanted. She turned to face him. "I'm a mess. I'm not the type of woman you date."

Bear turned to her, facing her. "How would you know what type of women I date?"

"The tall, beautiful kind, right? Women like

Jewell." Piper could see Bear with a woman like Jewell.

"I've dated all types of women. Women who interest me. What about you? What type of men have you dated?" Bear pushed a strand of hair that had escaped her braid over her ear.

"Academic types." She sighed. "Honestly, they were more interested in getting off than having a relationship."

"Ah," Bear said and took her hand. "I like you, Piper. I like your strength, even though you don't see it. I enjoy your company. And, I won't lie, the fact that you're an athlete is a big step in the right direction for me. I think you're sexy, but I will never, ever push you for more than you're able to give me. You have been through hell these last couple of days. A few stolen kisses and hand-holding will be enough for me until you're ready to go further." He held up a hand. "If you're interested in me, that is."

Piper stared at the man across from her. "I am interested, Bear. I feel an incredible attraction to you. What woman in her right mind wouldn't?"

"But?" he prompted her.

"But I feel like I'm disrespecting Christopher by . . ."

"Living?" Bear said the word after a long pause.

She nodded. "Yeah. "

"What would Topher say about that?"

She chuffed out a heavy breath. "He'd probably ask me if what I just said was logical or if I took a ride on the stupid loop to his office."

Bear squeezed her hand and chuckled a bit. "Is it logical?"

She shook her head. "No. I'm on the stupid loop. But it's still hard, being tempted and excited when he ... He won't ever have this again."

"I know." He leaned forward and kissed her softly. "No pressure. When you're ready."

"Thank you." She moved and leaned against him as they stared into the heavens. She hoped that Christopher could see her now, with Bear, and hoped he'd approve. Because she was very attracted to the man next to her.

CHAPTER 15

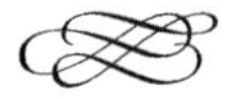

Bear shifted his weight and slipped under the blankets on the bed, but not under the sheet. The cave was freaking chilly at night. Piper moved in her sleep and turned toward him as he settled under the covers and closed his eyes. They'd sat outside for about an hour before returning to the cave and going to bed. Piper put on the t-shirt he'd given her the night before. He stared at the blackness of the cave above him. It was only last night that they'd found out that Christopher had been murdered.

He should be shot for kissing her, not only once but twice. So damn much had happened in such a short amount of time. *Compelled.* That was the word. He felt compelled to kiss her when they'd been together yesterday. Well, he needed to get his fucking compulsion under control. He didn't want to scare the woman off because what he was feeling for her was far outside the norm of what he'd felt for other women. And yes, some of that could have started from the fact that he was trying to keep her alive, but it wasn't all the inner caveman. She was so damn smart and beyond beautiful when she smiled. The pressure of the last few days had been intense for both of them. Perhaps that spiked his desire, but there was no doubt he wanted Piper.

And that was crass, wasn't it? He wanted to date her. Listen to him, acting like a high schooler. Holding hands and stealing kisses. But he considered what he knew about Piper. He didn't think it would be the wrong way to get to know her. He had no idea how long they'd be there, but while they were, he'd find a way to let her see he was a man of his word. The woman was entitled to time to mourn. He'd put away his desires and wants and let her heal, even if it meant he had to open a gym in Baton Rouge to be near her.

Bear rubbed his face and shook his head. He was such a …

"Why are you awake?" Piper whispered from next to him.

Crap. "Did I wake you?"

"No, I have to use the bathroom." She sat up and pushed the blankets off her. "It's cold in here. Are you warm enough?"

"I slipped under the blankets. Not the sheet, though."

Piper yawned and got out of bed. "Be right back."

The light for the bathroom turned on as she entered, but it was muted, which was interesting. The lighting strength must be on a timer or something. He waited for her to come back to bed. A moment later, she slid under the covers, her teeth chattering a bit. He pulled her close, and she snuggled up next to him.

"If I asked you to make love to me, would you?"

Bear stiffened and pulled away from her. "Excuse me? What?"

She tipped her head back. He could see her eyes until the light in the bathroom clicked off. "I want to feel something good. I'd be using you, I know, but I want to forget all the bad things that have happened. I want to feel good."

"This is a huge change from a few hours ago." He ran his fingers through her hair.

"Yes. I know." She put her hand on his chest. "I want something for me, and it's selfish, but I want you."

He heard her swallow hard. She was scared. Of him? Of being intimate so soon after they'd found out Topher had passed. He sighed and put his hand over hers. "And I won't deny I want you. I can't believe I'm saying this, but let's sleep on it. We'll take this further if you're still sure tomorrow." In his gut, he knew that was the right answer for Piper, not for himself. His over-active and suddenly teenaged libido was screaming to take her up on the offer.

"You don't want to?" she whispered.

Bear could hear the hurt in her words. He cupped her face in his hands and brought his lips to hers. "God, yes. I want to, I desperately want to, but I don't want you to regret asking me in the morning. Give it one day. Think about us together. I'm not the one-night-stand kind of guy, and from what I know about you, I don't think you're that type of woman. Am I right?"

She nodded but didn't say anything. Bear slid closer while pulling her to him. He wanted her to feel how much he wanted her. He moved his hips forward and knew when she felt his hard cock by the soft pulse of air from her lips. "I want you. Don't think I don't. What I *don't* want is regret ruining what could be between us." He kissed her again but didn't linger because he'd be second-guessing his decision to be a gentleman. "Go to sleep, Piper. I'm here. I'm watching over you, and I'll be here, in this bed, with you tomorrow night, and there won't be a sheet separating us." Bear held her as she relaxed and slipped into sleep. He truly hoped she wouldn't change her mind, but he'd feel like a complete ass if he hadn't asked her to be sure.

BEAR HEADED up the ramp to the makeshift office they'd been given. Sleep had been hit and miss last night. Mostly miss. Piper was sleeping when he finally gave up trying to sleep. He and Dude had gone outside, and he'd thrown a stick for the dog until his arm was rubber. The animal had stamina.

Zane was waiting for them when they finally came back into the cave. "Thanks for taking him out. This is the first time I've slept in since we picked him up. Coffee is ready."

"Thanks."

"So, where are you in the investigation?" Zane asked as they sat down at the table.

"Nowhere. We—and by we, I mean Piper—have an idea that whatever sent her brother to Washington has something to do with Freedom of Information Act requests. But we don't know enough about the process to know what it is."

"What do you need to know?" Jewell asked as she walked into the kitchen.

"Everything."

Zane got up, grabbed a cup for his wife, who sat at the table, and added creamer to the coffee before bringing it over. Bear took note of how Zane cared for her. It was noticeable. The man's protective vibe couldn't be missed.

Jewell smiled at her husband and kissed him when he set her coffee down. Then Zane moved to the refrigerator and started pulling out food for breakfast. "Well, I can tell you anything you may want to know. I've pulled thousands of FOIA documents from other agencies. Each agency has its way of processing the reports, but they all have to follow the Freedom of Information Act guidelines," Jewell said.

"What guidelines are those?" Bear took a sip of his coffee.

"Well, timelines, for one. They have twenty duty days to process the request unless it covers multiple offices in one agency or mass quantities of files. Then they can notify you of a delay but still have to process it. Normally, the reports section in each agency is responsible for compiling the response. Of course, they love the rule of nine, so you might never get the information if they can cram the disclosure into one of them."

"Tell him what the rule of nine is, babe," Zane said from the other side of the kitchen.

"Oh, sorry, I forget not everyone follows my logic. There are nine exemptions that agencies can use to deny giving you access. Classified material, which is self-explanatory. Protected by statute, which means the information isn't the agency's to release. It belongs to a contractor or is under the umbrella of another organization. Any request for information that governs the internal running of an organization. Trade secrets or financial information that can give someone else a competitive edge if disclosed. Draft documents or personal opinions. Invasion of personal privacy, impeding an ongoing investigation, and there are two more, but I can't remember them off the top of my head. I could look at what he has and see if I can make sense of it."

"That would be fantastic," Piper said as she walked in. "He kept circling the stamps."

"On all of the documents?" Jewell cocked her head. "That's strange. They'd be different if they came from different agencies."

Piper sat down at the table without looking at him, instead focusing her attention on Jewell. "Why would information on the movements of non-fissle uranium from other countries to this country be denied? I read news articles all the time about how many pounds of this or that material has disappeared from the former Soviet Union, or this facility is processing that amount of nuclear waste."

Jewell shook her head. "I don't know. The alphabet agencies are fickle. I usually go around them to get my information. But if you show me what you have, I can try to decipher it."

"Do you have time now?" Piper started to stand.

Jewell popped up. "I do."

"No, Jewell, no work until after breakfast."

Zane put a plate of eggs in front of her. "I hope poached eggs, toast, and sausage is good for everyone. My wife is notorious for forgetting to eat, so we put a few rules in place."

"That sounds good to me." Bear looked at Piper. "You?"

She glanced at him, then spoke to Zane. "Just one egg and toast for me, please?" Something was off. Why wouldn't she look at him?

"Done. Bear?" Zane asked as he broke an egg into the pan.

"I'll have whatever you're having."

"So, your brother was trying to get information on uranium shipments?"

"Yes." Piper nodded. "Where we're starting has been referenced numerous times. He believed there was enriched uranium in Venezuela about the time he was in Cuba with Bear."

Jewell stopped with her fork halfway to her mouth. "How did he validate that?"

"Medical records released by the Venezuelan government showed a spike in acute radiation poisoning that coincided with the information in the article," Bear answered. "Right?"

"Yes, that's correct. After a time, he started pushing for information from the DIA, specifically, but also the NSA and the Nuclear Regulatory Commission."

"Con worked for the NSA. He might have a better grip on their process for that information." Jewell finished chewing and added, "We'll video him in and talk about that before I start any classified work."

"Thank you. From what I see in his notes, he was certain he was getting the runaround. I think that caused him to sit back and look at the whole. I just need to see the information the way he saw it. Right now, we're missing something. Something he saw that sent him to Dr. Franklin."

"Has Dr. Franklin been interviewed?" Zane asked as he sat a plate down in front of Piper.

"Jared should've taken care of that yesterday afternoon, but with the mess we left in DC, it could be today," Bear said. "I need to call him and find out how the people assigned to watch Piper are faring. Colten took a shot to the chest."

Zane grimaced as he set down plates for him and Bear. "We'll call him first. Then we'll get you in touch with Con."

Thank God. Four eggs, four pieces of sausage, and two pieces of toast. "Man, I think I love you," Bear said, digging into the food.

"Sorry, I'm taken." He tipped his head in his wife's direction as she laughed. Bear caught Piper side-eying him twice while he was eating. He didn't know what the issue was, but he'd find out as soon as they were alone.

Jewell and Zane's office reminded him of the bridge of a spaceship he'd seen in a movie. Everything was within arm's reach and curved around, so they had almost a three-hundred-and-sixty-degree work area. Monitors were everywhere. The small refrigerator at Zane's station was the only thing out of place.

"Jared first," Zane announced as he led them into a room with a conference table.

"Start the monitor," Jewell called to her husband. He'd already turned it on and winked at them.

"Done," he called back.

Jared appeared on the screen. "I'm glad you called. Dial Con into the video, please."

Jewell, who was just about to sit down, returned to the office.

Zane clicked on the image as soon as Con appeared. "He's on," Zane called to Jewell.

She was back and in her chair a moment later.

Jared leaned forward. "Archangel reached out

to the DIA. They have no record of Dr. Whitehead visiting or any appointments on Dr. Franklin's calendar, which doesn't support our assumption that he met with Franklin."

Con snorted. "He was in the building for seven minutes. I maintained a copy of the film I used to show his entrance. Here's a big surprise. The system I hacked into no longer has that day or the day after in the cloud. I shopped around. Nothing from any cameras, including traffic cams, in the area for those two days. Someone wiped them all out."

Jewell leaned forward. "We can find out who."

"I don't think so. I've worked it all night, toots. There's nothing to go on." Con ran his hands through his hair. "It's the cleanest wipe I've ever witnessed."

"Send it to me. I want to see." Jewell's request was more of a demand.

"I already have. It should be in your inbox. Brando has been working on it with me. We're stumped. If you find anything, you'll have to show us how."

"You know I will."

Piper spoke as soon as there was a break in the

conversation. "Wait, you're telling me they denied Christopher was there?"

Jared nodded. "In the beginning, yes. Then Con sent them the video footage that he'd retrieved. According to the Deputy Undersecretary for the DIA, all records had been altered. She's mad as a hornet and investigating. We know now from the Undersecretary that Dr. Franklin has been listed as being on vacation since the day before Dr. Whitehead arrived. Someone is trying to change the past."

"But they can't do that. What about the military member who escorted him into the facility?" Bear asked.

"As of right now, there's been no contact with that noncommissioned officer, and he's been reported as AWOL." Con typed as he spoke. "No movement on any credit cards. Not married, but a stellar NCO. His performance reports are all maxed out. Highly unusual behavior based on his past."

Jared shook his head. "I don't like this at all. Con, track down our military guy. If you need a team to look for him, tell Nic or Jade that you have my authority, and they'll make it happen."

"Speaking of teams," Bear interrupted.

"Ah, yes. Colten made it through surgery. He's in critical condition, but the doctors are optimistic. His partner, Ellen, was knifed in the back. She was dragged to the other side of the building and left in the bushes. She didn't make it." Jared choked up a bit when he conveyed that message.

"The men in the hall?"

Jared turned that over to Con. "We're working on that. It appears they have no connection and nothing that would link them together."

Jewell shook her head. "No affiliation? Financial? School? Work? Relation?"

"Nothing."

"Military or post-military employment?" Bear asked.

Con shook his head. "All prior military, no cross-over in assignments, I couldn't find any joint employment, but they all took jobs with some of these so-called security companies. Mercenaries, more or less."

Bear leaned forward. "There are US bases they could have passed through at the same time while working in that capacity."

Zane nodded. "That's right. They wouldn't associate much with the military at those bases, but the contracted security teams would stick together."

"I'll go back and look for anything I can find." Con started typing again.

Jared drummed his fingers on the desk. "That NCO would know everything we need to uncover. Where did he take Dr. Whitehead? Did he sign in, or is there a coverup going on?"

"He signed in," Con grunted. "You saw him in the video at the front desk writing something on that clipboard he was handed. Visitor logs are a strict requirement for a building where most everything is classified."

Bear nodded. He knew the procedures like everyone else that was in the military.

"What about Dr. Franklin? Maybe Christopher had called him and talked to him before that?" Piper asked.

Con's attention switched to another screen, or at least that was what it appeared to Bear as his head turned and he typed like a madman. "Dr. Whitehead made four calls to the DIA switchboard number in the forty-eight hours before he traveled to Washington."

"Assuming he was talking to Dr. Franklin, that would be something to check on." Jared nodded.

"Con, find out where the good doctor is vacationing."

"On it."

"May I add another thing?" Piper lifted her hand a little.

"Of course," Jared acknowledged.

She cleared her throat, "Did Christopher die the day he went to the DIA?"

Jared pulled a file over and flipped it open. "The medical examiners couldn't determine an exact time of death based on his exposure to water, but they believe it was close to that time, yes."

"And the NCO is missing," Piper added, almost talking to herself. "And I was targeted."

Jared nodded, and Piper continued, "So, someone is trying to erase Christopher's visit to DC."

"We believe they may have been trying to do just that. We need to uncover what sent Dr. Whitehead to Washington." Jared paused, then added, "Oh, Con, can you look at some documents? Piper and Bear think the link is some denied FOIA requests."

Con nodded. "Denied requests? Sure, I processed several when I was at the NSA."

Jared spoke again, "I'll leave you to it. Con, get me an address on Franklin and that NCO."

"As soon as humanly possible, boss man," Con said as he typed. "Can you scan the denial responses you want me to look at? I'll grab them as soon as they pop up."

"We're on it," Jewell said. "I'll get back to you on the wipe."

Con chuckled. "Good luck, toots. I will bow to your superior abilities if you can find anything."

"You wouldn't bow to anyone." Jewell snorted before she pushed a button and disconnected Con from the video. Jewell turned to Piper. "Do you have those reports?"

"In my bag. I'll go get them." Piper popped up and was out of the door before Bear could blink.

Bear stood and asked, "Do you want to scan them in here, or should we do it next door?"

"Next door. The scanner will transmit directly to Con." Zane spoke for Jewell, who had shoved a pencil in her mouth and was staring at the screen like something was on it, but it was blank.

She shook her head. "There has to be some evidence of the wipe. Something is there."

"You'll find it, babe." Zane stood and put his hand on her shoulder.

"What? Oh, right. I need to call up the ..." Jewell stood up and headed into the office.

"She's gone. When she's working on a problem or is in the zone, it's almost impossible to pull her attention to anything else." Zane sighed. "I'll come out and check on you and give you any updates we get."

"Thanks," Bear said before following Piper from the office area. He found her coming down the hall from the bedroom. "They want us to scan them in here. The documents that we scan will go straight to Con's workstation."

"Okay." Piper diverted and started pulling the loose papers out of her courier bag.

"Just a minute." He put his finger under her chin and lifted her face so he could look at her. "What's going on?"

"What? Nothing. Why?" She moved her chin and returned to pulling papers out of the bag.

He crossed his arms. "I'm not buying it, Piper. What changed since you fell asleep last night and this morning."

She hesitated and then shook her head. "Nothing." She started sorting the papers into stacks.

He took the pile of papers from her. "I call bullshit."

She flinched and frowned at him. "That's crass."

"It is, but it's true. If you don't want me in your bed tonight, you only have to say the words." Bear put the papers down on the table. "I understand if you've changed your mind."

"Sure, you do." She nodded and reached for the papers.

"Wait, what's going on?"

"Oh, nothing. I'm sure many women in the world would love to be rejected and told to think about it before they have sex with a guy."

Bear sat down on the table, which groaned under his weight. Piper made a move to reach around him, but he snagged her by the waist and pulled her between his legs. "I told you I wanted you. I showed you how I felt."

She nodded, not looking at him. He turned her chin, meeting her eyes. Then he leaned forward and kissed her. Not the type of kiss he'd given her last night while in bed. Instead, he employed every technique he knew. He nibbled on her lips until she opened them for him. His tongue danced with hers, and when she wrapped her arms around his neck, he pulled her in close. One hand cupped her bottom, and the other found the nape of her neck. The feel of the woman was heavenly. She molded into him, and he could have kept her there forever. But air became a necessity. He ended the kiss the same way he'd started it, nibbling on her lips, and when he lifted away, her lips were swollen, and her eyes were half-lidded. "I didn't tell you to wait to embarrass you. I told you to wait to ensure you had time to consider the implications. I'm not a one-night stand. I will be in your life after this. I will take care of you. I will protect you, and I will make love to you. But we're exclusive."

Piper shuddered against him. "I accept that."

He kissed her again and then loosened his hold on her. "Now, we go to work and find out what brought Topher to DC."

She nodded and relaxed her arms, letting them slide from his neck down his arms. "NSA denials first, then DIA's, then the regulatory commission's.

He leaned down and kissed her again before grabbing the stack of papers and handing them to her. "You divide them up, and I'll scan them in.

CHAPTER 16

Jewell stared at the screen and went over everything again. Con was right. There was nothing left by whoever cleaned the video. She hit her coms, saying, "Con, I've never seen anything like this."

"Are we on speaker?" Con asked.

"No." She stared at the screen. "I don't understand. This is impossible."

"No, it isn't. Listen, I didn't want to say this in the conference because I signed an NDA, and they could nuke my ass for telling anyone this, but the NSA has developed tech that does this. It's almost impossible to track."

Jewell glanced over at Zane, who was working on something of his own. "Almost?"

"Yeah. I'll send you the process, but toots, this means that the NSA is involved in a coverup."

"But of what? A visit? I don't understand why anyone would go to these lengths."

"Money, power, or greed," Con answered. "Brando doesn't know what I just told you. The less who do, the better."

"I'm damn good with my systems. They'd expect me to be able to find it."

"But not so quickly." Con cleared his throat. "If they suspect I gave you that information, I'll be arrested."

"What information?" She chuckled. "We're on the most secure system in the world. They aren't getting in here, and I'm not telling anyone. We can use the information but find a way to color it, so no eyes are on us." She glanced back at Zane, who was looking at her with a narrowed gaze. "Zane is the best at doing that. We take care of our own, Con. Never forget that."

"It should be in your system. Put Zane on coms with us. I've got documents populating from the scanner." Jewell clicked the coms from her earbud to the speaker in the room. She heard Con typing and then a pause. "Jewell, pop up our shared screen."

She hit a few keystrokes and then looked up at the screen on the wall. "This isn't usual. I've denied FOIA requests. This stamp? It's an inter-agency stamp. Let me see … no, Dr. Whitehead's request was specific for the information obtained by and known to the NSA. Why … Oh, hey, toots, look at this.

The screen enlarged the bottom of three requests. "These are NSA denial letters. Three more letters focused on the stamp appeared. "These are DIA letters." He enlarged them. "See anything similar?"

Jewell played Where's Waldo for a minute and then blinked. "Are those initials?"

"Every time I denied the report, I had to send it through my department's supervisor. My boss's boss. Each office concurred, or it was kicked back to me with specific modifications."

"Okay." Jewell was tracking. She leaned in and stared at the top of each box. "W.C.F. Those initials are at the top of the NSA and the DIA's denial letter."

"Go grab the Nuclear Regulatory Commission letters, they say … Wait, never mind, I have them coming in now. More letters popped up on the screen. "W.C.F.," Zane said as he moved forward.

"Could be V.D.F., V.D.P, W.D.P., or W.D.F." He stared at the screen. "The handwriting is crap."

"That's what Dr. Whitehead noticed, though, isn't it? Who is that person, and why would they have access to all three organization's reply processes?" Jewell stared down at her keyboard.

"Are all NSA, DIA, and NRC employees listed?"

"The ones who deal with paperwork are. We had people undercover. They weren't listed on the employment rolls."

"You check the NSA, I'll scour the DIA, and whoever gets done first, grab the NRC."

Jewell's fingers flew through the roster of names on the public website. Nothing. "Con, you have access to our governmental databases?"

"I do, but I don't need them. I'm in. Seems no one deleted my permissions over there."

Jewell sniggered but burrowed through the governmental alpha roster for the DIA. Winston Dean Franklin. "I have one that matches in the DIA." She put the name up on the screen.

"Winston D. Franklin," Con said the name before she could. "I have two other names. Victor Douglas Faison and Vickie D. Farrington.

"NSA?" Zane asked.

“On it.” Con tapped away as Jewell pulled up information on all of the names.

“Four names. “Wilma Franklin, Vincent Faruq, Wallace Fishburne, and Winston D. Franklin.

“He works as a consultant at the NSA and the NRC?” Jewell stared at the information Con populated on the screen they were sharing.

“He consults at both the NSA and the NRC and is employed at the DIA,” Zane repeated her words. He stood with his hands on his hips, looking at the information. “Could it be a legitimate denial?”

“I don’t think so.” Con kept typing. “Why would a part-time consultant be the person to finalize a department’s work? Besides, the letter is the aftermath. The work is done before the letter is ever drafted. The thing is, in all instances, exemption one was used in the verbiage. He highlighted the rationale for denial in each letter. The request letters are not requesting classified information. They specifically ask for non-classified information about the movement of non-fissle uranium in other countries. How would that information be damaging to the US?”

“I don’t know,” Zane answered. “Maybe he signed off on them because of his specialty?”

“Still, I don’t think so. A supervisor’s head

would roll if it were denied when it should have been approved. I can't see any career government employee allowing this shit to fly." Con shook his head. "I think we have our link, but I have no idea what the hell is going on."

Jewell shook her head. "Piper deserves to know why. Where are we on finding this guy?"

"I haven't started."

She looked back at Zane, who nodded. "I'll take it. You find that NCO."

"On it." Con and the shared screen disappeared.

Zane picked up his headset and put it on. "I'm calling Jared."

Jewell nodded. "I'm going to find this guy and then find out why the NSA is wiping out all the evidence."

Zane paused and looked at her. "Say what?"

"Long story involving information I shouldn't have, but believe me, I'm going use the information to the best of my ability."

"Go get 'em, babe."

Jewell nodded. That was the plan.

Bear stared at the letters that were on the table. "Are these the same initials as these?" He pointed to the letters scrawled on the small lines.

Piper grabbed her hair and leaned over the table as she examined the fourteen letters they had lined side by side and on top of each other. They could be. She grabbed the notebook with Christopher's depiction and found the right page for the first request. "He has VDP listed on this one." She moved to the next one. "WDF here." She glanced from the paper to the notebook. "I can see the similarity in writing. I think the initials are the same person."

"It is," Zane said from the doorway. Bear had heard him walk up, so he didn't jump, but Piper sure as hell did. She almost cracked him in the nose when her head whipped up.

Zane saw the near miss, and his eyes widened, but he continued, "Dr. Franklin. He consulted for the NSA and the NRC and is a full-time employee of the DIA."

"What do the initials mean?" Piper backed into Bear, and he placed his hands on her shoulders.

"According to what we've discovered, the senior department head must approve or deny the report. In all instances, Franklin did instead. We're treading lightly on this. We don't want anyone to know we've discovered what Christopher saw."

Piper looked at the letters on the table. "They were on different walls. They weren't lined up like this. That's why it took him so long to figure out the same person was denying him access to the information."

"But he figured it out, only he couldn't have known it was Franklin. He wouldn't have known that Franklin consulted at the NSA and the NRC."

"He went to Franklin for help." Bear squeezed Piper's shoulders.

She sighed heavily. "And it got him killed."

"But Franklin wasn't at the DIA that day," Bear reminded her.

"We're making sure that's actually a fact." Zane shoved his hand in his pocket. "We're taking nothing at face value. Congratulations to both of you. If you hadn't kept at it, we wouldn't have found this anomaly."

"But it's more than an anomaly. Someone killed Christopher." Piper's finger landed on one of the pieces of paper. "Someone is trying to kill me. The lady officer was killed, and the other one was shot. This is more than an anomaly." She was shaking under Bear's hands.

Zane nodded. "Yes, ma'am. You're most assuredly correct. We have the best and the brightest working on this, and we're doing it as quickly as possible without giving whoever is orchestrating this dance of smoke and mirrors knowledge that we are on to them. If we let them know, they'll be gone. We want to take down everyone."

"But someone is going to approach Franklin?" Bear asked.

Zane nodded. "Yep, you and Jared are heading to Sedona, where we've tracked him down. Jared's flying in to pick you up in the morning. By then, we'll have our people in place, and we'll monitor them as we act on any information Franklin gives us. There's more going on here than what has happened to Christopher, and Guardian will dig until there's nothing left to clean up."

"Is there anything we can do to help?" Bear felt Piper relax when he gently squeezed the back of her neck.

"Can you take care of Dude? We'll be pulling overtime until we reach a stopping point. He's good for a couple of hours. I just took him out."

"We can take him for a run." Piper looked back at him. "I could use one."

Bear nodded, and Zane visibly relaxed.

"Perfect. Sorry for not being a good host. Do you remember what I told you about the road down the mountain?"

"I do. It's safe to run on, and no vehicles will be coming here," Piper said.

"Right. Knock if you need us. Help yourself to anything in the kitchen." He left the doorway with Dude at his heels.

Piper turned around. "We're going to get answers." She smiled. "Too late, but at least we'll know why."

Bear cupped her face and dropped for a kiss. When he lifted his head, he pulled her into him and held her tightly. He wasn't so sure they'd get answers. The man could plead the fifth, or he could be a pawn in the game. Whatever Christopher had stumbled upon was far bigger than just a man trying to get information. Bear was usually on the tip of the spear, taking down the guilty. He'd never been at the back end, doing the leg work to make the case or working the specifics leading up to the takedown.

Piper leaned back. "Can you run?"

Bear jerked and looked down at her. "Ah, yeah. Why?"

"No, can you run for miles?"

"Ten is my top, but we'd need to drag Dude by that time."

Piper smiled. "We wear him out, and then we run." She backed away from him. "Can you keep up?"

Bear narrowed his eyes. "Woman, if you want sex tonight, do not make me run more than ten miles."

Piper's eyes widened, and the small smile morphed into a larger one. "Ten miles it is." She turned and headed out the door. "Unless you want to do something else first, and we run later. Dude is set for a couple of hours."

It took Bear about half a second to register the implied invite. He was out of the room in an instant.

CHAPTER 17

Piper listened to Zane explain what was going on. Their computer techs had deciphered what Christopher had found at the same time as they had. She didn't care who found it. From her perspective, there was so much more going on. Zane has said as much, but what happened next was out of her area of expertise. She'd leave that to Guardian. Piper wanted justice. There was no doubt about her desire to exact justice for her brother. She wanted Christopher's murderer arrested, tried, and incarcerated for the rest of his life. But the relief that there was a way forward was profound.

She tuned back into the conversation when Bear said, "We can take him for a run."

Piper looked back at Bear and nodded. "I could use one." Bear knew that exercise was a coping mechanism for her. The medication was a wonderful addition, but she loved running. Bear smiled down at her and then nodded in Zane's direction.

Zane smiled. "Right. Knock if you need us. Help yourself to anything in the kitchen." He left the doorway with Dude at his heels.

Piper turned around. So much had happened in such a short amount of time. But she was happy. "We're going to get answers." Then the realization hit her. Not in time to help Christopher. She smiled sadly. "Too late, but at least we'll know why."

Bear cupped her face and dropped for a kiss. He took her breath away. For someone so big, he was gentle, almost too careful, but he could kiss. Her insides heated, and she wanted more of him. More than a kiss. But that was supposed to be his call to make. At least according to her plan that morning when she was getting ready. Piper had had a long talk with herself. Her medication had taken the edge off her anxiety, and she wished she'd had the regiment of medication years ago. It was almost like someone had taken the dark, depressing tint off her vision of the world. The medication didn't make losing Christopher any easier. His death would leave a gaping hole in her life, but he wouldn't want her to push away her life because he lost his. Christopher was a realist, and she didn't want to disrespect his memory or loss. Being intimate with Bear wouldn't do either of those things. Her life would continue.

Christopher would be utterly astounded that it took days for her to figure that out. She could see him; his eyebrow lifted, giving her that look. Yeah, she'd been sidetracked on the stupid loop. Lord, her brother had a way of making her laugh, and she'd miss that so much.

The simple revelations she'd had were her map, giving her a way to go forward. She'd honor him and his memory while still carrying the loss. But she needed to do that while living her life. She *could* have a relationship with Bear, she'd decided as she'd dressed. The one thing she was sure of was that Christopher would be bent out of shape if either she or Bear were hurt.

Still, she'd been a bit nipped over the fact that Bear had turned her down the night before, embarrassed, actually. She hadn't even known if she could even face him when they woke up. Talk about mixed signals. He wanted her but wanted to wait. Yeah, she understood his rationale, but she felt like a dolt for asking him to make love to her.

She'd shook her head and eyed herself in the mirror. "Why is this so hard?" *Because you have no idea how to move forward with this problem. You have little reference and even less experience.* Which was true. Well, the answer was that Bear would have to make the next move, wouldn't he? And he had. Leaving the ball in her court.

Well she'd played her shot. She'd given him the opportunity and volleyed the ball back across the net. Bear chased her from the office to the doorway of the bed room after she'd suggested they find alternate activities while Dude was good to go for a couple hours. He turned her around and his eyes searched hers like he was looking for the meaning of life. "Are you sure?" His voice was deep. God it sent a chill down her spine, but damn it, if she wasn't sure she wouldn't have said it. Piper lifted her eyebrow the way Christopher used to do to her. "Are you taking a trip on the stupid loop?"

Bear tossed back his head and laughed. "I might be." He moved them into the room and kicked the door shut with his foot. "But I'm on the right track now."

Piper wrapped her arms around his neck and walked backward as he walked forward. Bear's lips held hers captive, and she let him maneuver them toward the bed. She concentrated on the sensation of his lips and tongue. She'd been kissed before, but with Bear, it was a whole-body experience. His hands explored, his legs pressed against her, and his kiss … Lord, that kiss moved through her. It ignited a nuclear detonation that nothing else had ever come close to. Her body ached, and she rubbed her legs together, looking for some relief from the need growing inside her.

As she pushed up his shirt, he broke the kiss and whipped it off. Then he stared at her and started unbuttoning her shirt, but she shook her head and stepped back, taking it off the same way he'd removed his. When he unfastened his jeans, she mimicked his action, and after she'd stepped out of her jeans, she waited for him to remove his boots and take off his denim. His body was spectacular. He was thick and muscled in the chest and shoulders. His abs were tight and cut. As he removed his boxers, the deep V that appeared led to his shaft. It was hard and pointed straight at her.

She'd never had the opportunity to admire a male form before, and God, there was so much to admire with Bear. His tattoos covered one arm and shoulder, like a warrior's plating from the ancient Roman era.

She reached behind her and popped the clasp of her bra, letting it fall from her shoulders to the ground. She'd never been ashamed of her body, and her running kept her fit and trim. Still, there was hesitancy, but she couldn't let him see. He'd make her wait again, and the hesitancy wasn't about the sex. Her mental hesitation came from her curiosity about how she would compare to the other women.

She shimmied out of her panties and stood there, staring at him. He moved toward her and pulled her into his arms. His hot skin branded her as they came together in another blistering kiss. The ridge of his shaft was hot and hard against her abdomen as he backed her up until her legs hit the bed. He broke the kiss, swept her in his arms, and lifted her onto the bed. He was over her at the same moment. His kiss didn't deter her hands, which she ran over his arms and shoulders. She grasped at his back when his hand slid down her stomach to her core. She opened her legs, and he positioned himself between them.

He broke the kiss and stared down at her. "Protection?"

She reached up and cupped his face. "I have an IUD."

He lowered and kissed her again, whispering, "Tell me again you want this."

"I want you," she answered and rose to meet his lips, shutting him down from asking any more questions.

Bear's hesitation seemed to dissolve with those three words. He traveled her body with his hands and mouth, and she grasped the blanket on the bed when he kissed her. The sensation was unlike anything she'd ever experienced. Her hips lifted, and he wrapped his arms around her legs, pinning her to the bed as he did things to her that she'd never imagined. Her legs clenched, and her body tightened. The sensation seemed to echo within her. Piper grasped his hair and cried out when it happened again, but that time, her muscles convulsed, and the echo rolled through her. She stared down at him. Lord, whatever that was, she wanted it to happen again.

He lifted and smiled a wide, happy grin that

reminded her of the Cheshire cat. He licked his way back up, stopping to excite her nipples. The act seemed to have a direct impact on her sex. The echo was gone, but the need for more wasn't.

He slid his arms under hers and aimed his cock at her center. As Bear rocked into her a little bit at a time, Piper's hips moved to meet his thrusts. She tightened her fingers in his hair and pulled him down to her. She wanted more of him. More of his kisses, his touches, and more of *him*. The sensations as he filled her were hard to explain. The way he touched her, kissed her, and treated her was with care, but that, that was primal. When they broke for air, she stared up at him. The muscles of his neck and shoulders strained under his skin. His veins were more pronounced, and a sheen of perspiration covered him. She slid her hands up his arms, and he looked down at her. Their eyes locked for a moment, and she wished she had the words to explain how monumental it was for her. But words weren't an option anymore. She arched under him. "Please." She couldn't articulate any other word. He dropped to one elbow and hooked his other arm under her leg. He lifted it and withdrew before returning with a fast stroke.

God, yes, that was what she needed. "More."

She grasped his shoulders with her fingers and squeezed as tight as she could. Bear moved his hips faster, and the strokes were stronger. That echo feeling started to roll inside her. Almost there. She could feel the tightening as if a string was being pulled back. The need for that release was mind-boggling and the only thing she could think about. "More, please."

"I've got you. I'll take care of you." Bear shifted and lifted to his knees. Lifting her legs, he hilted. His skin glistened with sweat, and his neck and shoulders were straining. She closed her eyes and concentrated on the sensations building. She grabbed the blankets with both fists and lifted her hips as he thrust in. The string tightened again. She arched, and he drove into her. The snap reverberated through her, stronger than the first time. Piper groaned as the clenching spasm destroyed her in the best possible way. She grabbed the blankets and held on as Bear finished and dropped to his elbows over her. They panted momentarily until he rolled to his side and tugged her with him.

She flopped onto his chest and laughed, "You're sweaty."

"Right back, attcha." He grunted the words and

lifted her hair. It fell to her back, damp from her perspiration.

"I think we should do that again." Piper's head lifted and fell at his laugh.

"Give me a minute to catch my breath."

She lifted her head and looked down at him. "Only a minute. You see, it's necessary. All experiments must be repeated to ensure the same outcome is achieved. If not, it's a fluke, requiring more experimentation."

"This wasn't a fluke." As his hand traveled up her back to the nape of her neck, a shudder traveled through her body. "But I'd be happy to experiment again." He rolled her to her back. "And again." He dropped a kiss on her shoulder. "And again."

CHAPTER 18

His legs were fucking rubber, but he would finish the run or die trying. Beside him, Piper's stride was perfection. Longer than he thought it would be, he could easily match her stride by shortening his a bit. They fell into a rhythm. Of course, because they were on top of a fucking mountain, they ran downhill first, only to turn at the bottom and run back up the damn thing. He could see the garage, their starting point.

Once they'd reached it, he stopped and grabbed his knees. Fuck, he was all in. She put her hand on his back. "Walk it off, soldier."

"Not a soldier." He straightened. "A SEAL."

Piper grabbed his hand. "I stand corrected. Come on, Mr. SEAL. Walk it off."

Bear held her hand as they cooled down. "Are you okay staying here while I go with Jared?"

Piper looked at him and then nodded. "Dude will keep me company, I'm sure. I know they have work to do, so I'll try to be helpful and stay out of the way."

"I don't like leaving you." She was *his* to protect. *His* to watch over.

"I'll be okay … You're coming back, right?"

Bear snapped his head to look at her. "Of course. Why do you ask?"

She shrugged. "The reason we're together is over. We figured out what brought Christopher to Washington."

He stopped and tugged her to him. "The reason we began this trip together is over. The reason we're together, here and now, has just started." He dropped a firm kiss on her lips. "Don't confuse the two."

She opened her eyes and then smiled up at him. "Right answer."

"Were you testing me, professor?" He traced her bottom lip with his finger. God, he could feast on her lips and live on nothing but her taste. They had chemistry beyond anything he'd had with anyone else. He wasn't exaggerating on that point.

His undeniable attraction to her was special to him because of it.

She cocked her head to the side. "Maybe. It's nice to know you feel the same way I do."

Bear nodded to a big boulder. "Let's have a seat for a second." She did a double take at him and nodded. He took both her hands in his. God, he hoped he put it in the right way. "Piper, I'm not used to expressing my emotions. I've learned to internalize them." He shrugged. "Call it macho, alpha-warrior training, or the fact that I'm not usually around people I care for ... whatever. Unfortunately, sometimes I don't say what I'm supposed to say. Not because I don't feel what you're feeling, but because I don't even think to express my feelings. I will try to be better about opening up, but I want you to know straight off the bat that I want a relationship with you. I don't want this, what's between us, to end when you go back to Baton Rouge."

She blinked a couple of times. "You're making me misty." She sniffed. "Stop that."

He chuckled. "I apologize."

She sniffed again. "I feel the same way. But long-distance relationships are hard."

He cupped her cheek. "So, we don't do that."

"It isn't that easy." She shook her head and sighed.

"Yes, it is. I move to Baton Rouge. I can start a gym anywhere."

"You'd do that? For me?"

"Yes. Any man worth his salt will make accommodations for the special someone in his life. If you don't finish your doctoral program and find a job somewhere teaching at a college, I'll open a gym in that city." He stopped. "If you'd want that. I don't want to pressure you."

Piper leaned into his hand. "I want that."

"Then we'll finish what brought us here. I'll come back for you, and we'll figure out the future. One step at a time." He kissed her again. God, he couldn't get enough of the woman.

He helped her off the boulder and headed back up to the cave. "I meant to ask you earlier, why are you going with Jared?" Piper glanced over at him as she spoke.

"He promised to let me in on the takedown." He would love to see Franklin crack under Jared's interrogation techniques.

"What if Franklin wasn't there?"

"He still has a lot of explaining to do. Why was he declining all of Topher's requests? We've read them. Most of them should have been approved—the documentation given to Topher through the Freedom of Information Act. The denial will need to be explained at a minimum."

When the door opened, Dude launched at Piper. Bear snagged him just before he would have toppled her, and she laughed. "Remind me not to go for a run if someone isn't around to catch him. I think he wants to play again."

"We can throw the sticks for him, but I'm not running another step. Not if you're expecting anything except snoring tonight." Bear grabbed her hand and turned. Dude barked and bolted down the path. He understood the word stick because he grabbed one and sprinted back to Bear. He dropped it, his tail going a million miles an hour. Bear chucked it, and Dude flew after it.

"Do you think it'll be safe for me to return to Baton Rouge?" Piper leaned against a tree and watched as he threw the stick for Dude each time he brought it back.

Bear glanced in her direction. "I'm going to do everything in my power to make sure it is." He'd asked himself the same question. It would be one of the answers he'd get from Jared King before taking Piper off the mountain. If she was in danger, they'd find a way to stay off the grid without inconveniencing Zane and Jewell. He'd change his name or whatever he needed to do to keep her safe. His brother would be okay. The man had a rich career ahead of him. Bear had made sure Wolf had the best he could provide.

Piper laughed when Dude brought back a bigger stick. He threw the mini-log, and the dog barked, running after it. He looked at her as he waited for Dude to come back. "Are you okay?"

She jerked her attention from where Dude was searching for the stick. "Huh?"

"Are you okay?" He repeated the question, worried she might be internalizing her fears and building to a panic attack.

She cocked her head. "Oh, you mean anxiety-wise?"

He nodded and grabbed the stick that Dude deposited at his feet. "My man, the concept of fetch is you bring back the *same* stick." He whipped the new twig, and Dude flew after it.

He turned to Piper, giving her his undivided attention as she walked over to where he was and put her hand on his chest. "I wish I'd taken the everyday medication my doctor prescribed years ago. I don't feel the constant doom and worry. So,

I'm okay there. I am okay with us. Better than okay. I'm good with you going with Jared. I'm still grieving Christopher, and that hits hard at the most random times." She gave him a small smile. "I'm sure that will continue to happen for a long time. Just come back for me."

Bear would take out anything that tried to block him from returning to her. "Wild horses couldn't keep me away." Guns, mortars, tanks, legions of kick-ass warriors. You name it; he'd take them on, send them to hell, and keep coming.

Dude bounded through the trees toward them. "Let's wear this guy out. Then we can take a nice, long shower and make dinner for all of us." Piper leaned into him. "I want to experiment some more."

Bear laughed. "Professor, you can use me as your test subject any time."

"Ah, a willing victim. Always better." She moved over to a large rock and sat on it as he threw the stick again. Oh, hell yes, he was willing. Able? That was another question. He laughed. He felt his stamina would be tested with Piper, and brother, he was up for the challenge.

AFTER MAKING sure Dude had water in his dish, Bear headed up the ramp to the room he shared with Piper. He heard the sound of the shower as he opened the door and decided he needed to jump in too. Whipping off his drenched clothes, he noted the salt and sweat stains might not ever come out. He put his clothes with Piper's. He'd throw them into the wash when they cooked dinner.

The shower was an architectural wonder. The floor had been carved into a slight depression, and the water ran off through a narrow channel chiseled into the rock. The rainwater shower head was large and square, and under its stream, Piper tipped her head back, working shampoo out of her hair. Bear reached for her and placed his hands on her hips. She smiled but kept her eyes closed. He held her as she leaned back farther. The soap spilled down her shoulders and trailed across her skin. His cock was ready to go even though his legs felt like pudding. He didn't care. He was making the most of their time together. When she lifted, he kissed her. The combination of her soft skin under his hands and her wildly addictive flavor in his mouth shored up his tired legs. He would take her if he had to jack up his ass with a hydraulic lift.

She backed out of the water and grabbed the

soap. She started washing him. Lord, in heaven. The feel of her hands on him was so fucking sensual. She didn't shy away from his body, and she didn't appear shy about hers either. He got that. Athletes knew their bodies were strong and fit. He hissed when her soapy hand cupped his hard-as-a-diamond cock. She paused and then did it again. He shuddered and grabbed her hand. "Woman, if you want to repeat the experiment, you better stop."

Piper's laugh was unexpected but sounded beautiful. "Maybe I want to conduct a new experiment." She stroked him again.

"It won't take much." He was honest. He was primed. The woman did it for him on so many levels. Athletic, sexy, and genuine, damn, Piper was his, and that possessive streak was new for him. It had been developing since he'd met the woman when he thought she was fragile. But she'd proven she wasn't. Through all her difficulties, she'd proven she was strong, capable, and so damned determined. And those attributes were just as sexy as her tight body, big brown eyes, and luscious lips.

Making a humming sound, she continued to stroke his cock, and he closed his eyes and dropped his head back. The water fell, warm and soft, and Piper's hand cupped, moved up his shaft, swirled around the head of his cock, and stroked back down. She cupped his balls in her hand, and his head whipped forward. He steadied himself by putting his hands on Piper's shoulders. The next stroke, he shot.

His hearing and sight did a momentary reboot because, damn, that orgasm shook him to his core. When he opened his eyes, Piper stared up at him, her bottom lip trapped by her teeth. She released it and smiled. "You liked that."

He chuffed out what little air was in his lungs. "I did."

"I made you feel good." She tipped her head to the side as if that revelation was new.

"You make me feel fantastic every time we're together." He bent down to kiss her. "Now, it's my turn to make you feel good." He sank to his knees. The hard rock of the shower floor be damned, he was going to rock her world.

Her hands worked through his wet hair as he worshipped her body. She was extraordinary and so responsive to his touch. As he explored her, he noted what made her shiver, what she leaned into, what she pulled away from. He learned what she liked and where her erogenous spots were. He wasn't in any rush. They had nowhere to be, and no one expected anything from them. It was just them at that moment. Bear sat back on his heels and pulled her closer, centering on her sex as he lifted her leg over his shoulder and gave special attention to what she liked. He wrapped one arm around her and used the fingers of his free hand to aid in stimulating her. She arched her back, and he held her upright. Her position was precarious, but he'd never let her fall. The fact that she trusted him so explicitly shattered any reserve he had left with her. The woman slayed him with her trust. He was a goner.

He felt her contract around his fingers, and knowing she was close, he pulled her clit into his mouth, nibbling just the slightest bit. She curled forward, her body shaking as she orgasmed. He licked his way to her hip and kissed her there as he let her leg down but still held her up. She leaned into him, her shaking hands found his hair, and she tangled through it. "God, that was … so, so good."

Bear lifted into a standing position while still holding her. They stood under the warm water, holding each other for some time. He heard her stomach grumble. "Your stomach is talking to us.

Dinner time." He reached behind her and turned off the water.

"Bear?"

He turned to her, offering her a towel. "Yes?"

"Is it always this good for you?" She wrapped the towel around her. "I don't mean to be rude by asking, but this is so much better than before with others. For me, I mean." She sighed. "The question sounded better in my head."

He finished wrapping the towel around his waist. "This, between us, is better than my past experiences. This is special." He kissed her, wrapping his arms around her.

When he lifted, she sighed and leaned into him. "I hoped it was." Her stomach grumbled loudly. Bear laughed when she leaned away from him and looked at her stomach. She put a hand over the towel. "Stop ruining my moments, will you?"

"We need to fuel up. We've expended a lot of calories today." Bear took her by the hand, and they moved into the bedroom. He stopped and leaned down once again to kiss her. "I promise many, many more moments in the future."

CHAPTER 19

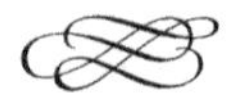

Piper sat on one of the large boulders outside the cave, watching Dude sniff about. Zane and Bear had left about an hour ago, so she supposed he was almost to the airstrip. She looked up as Jewell came out, walked over to the boulder, and sat on it with her.

"How long have you and Bear been together?" Jewell handed her a bottle of water.

"Ah, we just met, actually."

Jewell's head snapped around. "Say what, now?"

"Yeah, I called him when I became desperate to find Christopher." Piper opened the bottle of water.

"Why on earth didn't you say something when I put you in one room? Oh, man, that must have been uncomfortable for you. I am so sorry. I don't read people well. Geesh ... I'm ... damn, I'm sorry."

Piper felt her face flush but admitted, "Well, we didn't mind. We're ... dating?" Piper cocked her head and gave Jewell a quizzical stare. "Sleeping together. He wants more, and so do I. Is that dating?"

Jewell sighed and opened her water. "I think so, but I'm not good with people. Computers, I understand. Usually, Zane has to decipher people for me." She sighed. "He's the best thing to ever happen to me."

"Bear has seen me at my worst. I suffer from extreme social anxiety and wasn't taking my medication correctly. My doctor had recommended I take daily doses in the past, but I thought I knew better. But I'm on a regimen now, and it's so much better, but I had a panic attack the night the house was set on fire. He took care of me through that. He was there when I collapsed after identifying Christopher's body."

Jewell winced. "I can't imagine what you went through—what you're going through. I lost my dad when I was young. That was the reason I started working with computers. They made sense. Nothing else did. But now I have Zane, and I understand my family and mom and dad better."

"Wait, you have another dad now? Your mom remarried?"

"Oh, yeah. He's wonderful, and if I could have hand-picked someone for my mom, it would have been Frank. He adores Mom and treats her like she's his queen." Jewell sighed. "That's what I have with Zane. No matter how difficult I am, and believe me, I know I'm not an easy person to deal with, especially when I get lost in work, he's there, and he loves me. He's never tried to change me. Limit my work and make me eat healthy food, yes, but he hasn't asked me to be anything but what I am. I'm so lucky to have him."

Piper nodded and thought back to her limited time with Bear. He'd never once criticized her for her anxiety. That was what she'd expected, but he hadn't been like her father or, to a lesser degree, her mother. "When people don't understand what's going on in another person's brain, they try to apply their perspective to the situation."

Jewell nodded. "Exactly. People called me toxic. Zane saw through that. He saw me. That's pretty extraordinary when that special someone sees you for who you are and loves you all the more because of it."

Piper nodded. "I really like Bear. He's different from the men I've known before."

Jewell leaned back and laughed when Dude chased a squirrel through the underbrush. "He's not the brightest dog."

"He's still a puppy. How big do you think he'll get?" Piper laughed when Dude stood on his hind legs and barked at the squirrel.

"Zane says at least six or seven inches taller and about a hundred and fifty pounds when fully grown."

Piper snorted. "He'll be able to knock anyone over."

Jewell nodded. "It's why we got him. He's here to protect me from squirrels, skunks, and anyone stupid enough to come up the mountain if Zane is gone. But as long as Zane is here, I never have to worry about anything like that. Men like Zane and Bear are born to be protectors."

Piper nodded and smiled at Dude, who had just realized Jewell was outside. The dog came bounding up to her, his tail wagging like a whip. "I better get back to work." Jewell stood and wiped off some of the doggy kisses. "Thanks for the visit."

Jewell smiled and stroked Dude's coat. "You're easy to talk to. We should keep in touch after you leave."

"I'd like that." Piper watched as Jewell headed back into the cave with Dude padding along beside her. She took a breath and stared at the wilderness. "Christopher, I miss you." She sighed and looked down at her hands. "But I'm going to push forward. I really like your friend Bear. You were right to trust him." Piper sighed, stared at the blue skies, and watched as the white clouds hung in pristine relief against the backdrop of the mountains. It was a beautiful place to deal with losing her brother and to wait for Bear to return. She closed her eyes and smiled, enjoying the warmth of the sun on her skin. Bear would come back, and then they'd figure out the next step.

"Is that the turn?" Bear pointed to a turnoff.

Jared slowed down, and they both looked at the GPS. "Looks like it." He made the turn, and the SUV they were driving trundled down the rutted road. "How in the hell did you find him out here?" Bear and grabbed the dash as the SUV bottomed out in one of the ruts. "These tracks are new. It must have rained recently and been torn up when it was wet." Bear was a hell of a tracker, he'd learned while serving, but damn, the ruts were so deep a kindergartener could read them. "Several trucks both in and out." He could see two sets of tire tracks. Big treaded tires and deep, which meant they were heavy.

"There." Jared pointed to an old house. They had to slow to almost a crawl but managed to drive to the house without ripping the oil pan off the bottom of the vehicle. There were several outbuildings around the old place. What was missing was a vehicle.

Bear glanced around as he got out. "Footprints." Deep and everywhere. "A lot of people here recently. At least six."

Jared walked around the back of the SUV. "No car."

"Did Franklin rent one?"

Jared nodded. "A black Pathfinder."

"Could be in one of the outbuildings." Bear nodded in the direction of two that would hold a vehicle.

"Let's see if he's here." Jared mounted the steps, and Bear followed, keeping his eyes open as Jared knocked on the door and waited. There was no sound except for an occasional bird or insects flitting by.

Jared looked in the window and leaned back. "Looks quiet." He tried the door. It was unlocked. Jared pushed the door open, and Bear drew the weapon from the holster on his leg and followed Jared into the house.

Jared's gun was drawn, and he motioned for Bear to go right. Jared went left. They worked to clear the small first floor. The stairs were to the second floor were old, and the noise of their arrival would have awakened the dead, but fortunately for them, there were no dead upstairs. Clothes were still in the bedroom, Franklin's, he assumed. A bathroom kit was open on the tiny vanity, and the toothbrush was hanging in the holder.

They walked down the stairs, and Jared pulled out his phone. "Con, he's not here."

Jared put the phone on speaker. "His phone is pinging from that location. Hold on, let me check again."

"Yep, hold on. I'm calling it."

A muffled sound of a cell phone ringing sounded. Bear and Jared moved into the living room, and Bear dropped to his knees and pulled the phone from underneath the couch. "Interesting." He tossed it to Jared.

"Con, anything on the rental?"

"Also at your location, according to the onboard computer system."

Bear walked out onto the porch. "Let's take a walk."

"We'll call you back." Jared hung up, and they rounded the corner of the house. "Oh, damn. Do you smell that?" Bear knew that smell. Something was dead. There was no other smell that even remotely came close to the stench of a rotting body.

Jared pulled out his automatic. Bear hadn't holstered his. They moved upwind. The putrid smell of death grew stronger. They opened the door of a small shed, and Bear held his breath as he went in before backing out almost immediately. "Fuck. I'm not sure who it is, but he's wearing a battle dress uniform. I don't know which branch."

Jared covered his mouth and nose with a handkerchief and looked in. "Sweet Jesus."

Bear moved to the side of the building to get some fresh air. The body had been chopped apart.

An ax was in the man's skull, and his legs and arms had been hacked off. Jared joined him for fresh air.

"How strong is Franklin? Jesus, there's something off here. The person who did that to the man acted in hatred or anger. That wasn't a normal killing." Bear spit, trying to get the coating of stench from his throat.

"I think that's our missing NCO. The one who took Dr. Whitehead back at the DIA."

Bear nodded. That made sense. "But where's Franklin?"

Jared motioned to the other outbuildings. "My guess."

"Let's do it." Bear moved forward, keeping his eyes out for any movement whatsoever. The remoteness of the location made it a perfect killing ground. There weren't any neighbors for miles.

"This one." Jared moved left. He went right. They cleared the outside of the windowless building before they tried the door. It was locked. Bear holstered his weapon and pulled out his wallet, removing the lock picks from the binding of the leather. He slid in the first tool, added the second, and manipulated the simple lock. It clicked open not more than fifteen seconds later. He put his wallet away, palmed his weapon, and stood.

Jared nodded, and Bear twisted the knob. The door swung open. When they entered, he went low, and Jared went high. It was an office. There were two computers on the desk. A series of ledgers and a multitude of notes pinned to the wall were reminiscent of Topher's bedroom. They walked into the small building, and Bear stared at the items on the wall. "They're the same documents Topher had posted in his office. He glanced down at the desk. "Look."

Jared glanced down. "Okay, what am I looking at?"

"Franklin's notes. Block lettering. No script."

"Fuck." Jared sighed. "Someone was declining the reports, and it wasn't Franklin. The initials were written in script."

"Flowery script." Bear nodded. "I'd bet my life savings that one of these computers is Christopher's. He probably gave it to Franklin when Franklin denied declining the reports."

"Shit is getting deeper and deeper." Jared pulled out his phone and dialed. "Con put a red ribbon around this place. Get authority from Archangel. Send in a team from Phoenix and do it immediately. This place must be processed before any locals get wind of what's happening."

"I'd be happy to do so if you could tell me what's going on." Con sounded a bit confused.

"We don't know the extent yet. Tell Archangel I said the scene needs a red ribbon. He'll understand." Jared's clipped command held no room for debate.

"You got it."

Jared slid the phone into his pocket. "Next building?"

Bear nodded, and they moved across the open expanse to the next building. It, too, was windowless. There were double doors, but they'd been wedged shut from the outside. Bear moved the pieces of wood. He lifted one for Jared to see. Blood. It was done with the ax that had killed the NCO. That meant the skull blow was delivered after someone had chopped those two pieces of wood. That was one sick motherfucker.

They each grabbed a door handle.

Jared mouthed, "One, two, three."

They pulled the doors open. Bear went low, Jared high. The black Pathfinder was parked in the building. They moved as one clearing the building before turning to the truck because, instinctively, they knew it wasn't a threat. A plastic tube ran from the exhaust to the passenger side window.

Duct tape kept the tube around the muffler, and the opening in the window kept air from entering the car's cabin.

The person he assumed was Dr. Franklin was sitting in the driver's side seat, slumped to the side. The vehicle had stopped running, but it was evident that the man had died from asphyxiation.

Jared called Con back. "Send me a picture of Dr. Franklin." Jared hung up.

"There's a note," Bear said, pointing to the seat.

"Convenient," Jared grunted and held up his phone. He looked at the dead man. "This is Franklin."

Jared's phone vibrated, and he read it. "We have the case. Our prints will be excluded from the crime scene, but let's get the kit. It's been a hot minute since I've processed a scene, and we need to do this by the numbers."

Bear nodded. Yeah, the butchers made a statement. "Just tell me what to do. I'm damn good at following instructions." Bear walked with him back to the Guardian SUV.

"You get the camera. I want everything photographed, and I'll need your statement about where you found Franklin's phone. We should have left it there. Rookie mistake on my part."

"Oh? Were you expecting a double homicide?" Bear snorted.

"Not really, no," Jared admitted. "And you said two homicides. What makes you believe that Franklin didn't kill himself?"

"The doors wedged from the outside for one." Bear glanced at Jared. "That's enough, right?" He so wasn't a cop.

"It's a big indicator." Jared agreed. "Did you notice his hands?" Jared put on a pair of latex gloves and handed a pair to Bear.

"No, why?"

"Three of his fingernails had been pulled out."

"Fuck. Torture?" Whoever these motherfuckers were, they needed to be ended.

"This looks like rage, not predictive actions. I'm not sold that they were anything but lowlife criminals hired to take these guys out."

Bear turned to look toward the small outbuilding. "That's why they didn't take the computers."

Jared nodded. "Yes, my initial thoughts. But the investigation will tell us more. We'll process Franklin's scene first."

Bear followed Jared back to the building and placed markers where he was told to place them. He took photographs, logging the date, time, and approximate location of each of the photographs, and then triangulated measurements of the vehicle as Jared dusted for prints on the outside of the vehicle. There were hundreds.

"Probably not the perp's," Jared said as he worked. "It's a rental. This is a child's handprint. God only knows how many people touched this vehicle." Bear continued to fetch and tote for Jared. Finally, the man stood up and straightened his shoulders. "We're going to open the door. Photograph Franklin from as many angles as you can. I'll hold a ruler to show his position in the seat. Pay particular attention to the condition of his clothes."

"Why?" Bear asked as he started to work.

"The rain," Jared reminded him. Bear took a wide-angle shot that got all of Franklin in the frame. His pants were muddied. It looked like he'd fallen several times. Bear leaned in and took more photos, careful not to touch anything. The top of the man's shoes was caked in mud, but there was a definitive direction of the way the mud had dried. As if the man had been … "They dragged him through the mud."

Jared nodded. "I don't doubt that he was unconscious when they put him in the truck.

Otherwise, he would have gotten out. The doors weren't locked."

"Unconscious from them pulling his fingernails out." Bear stood up. "Where would they have done that?"

Jared sighed and looked out of the building they were working. "My gut tells me they made Franklin watch the young NCO as he was killed. We'll probably find his fingernails on the ground in the shed."

"Jesus, Jared, what type of person does this kind of shit?"

"You know exactly what type." Jared rolled his shoulders. "My question is, who are they working for? What's the end game?"

Bear straightened. "Do you hear that?" There was a definite thrum in the air.

"That would be the Phoenix crew." Jared stepped out of the building to see a helicopter landing in a field far enough away from the house that no prop wash reached the area. Four men ran from the helicopter in a crouch carrying bags.

As they approached, one spoke, introducing themselves. "Mr. King. Ray Quantell. My team and I are ready to go. What do we have?"

Jared took the team to the shed, where the

military member was dismembered. "We also expect the victim in the vehicle was tortured here. A thumbnail, pointer finger, and middle fingernail were pulled out. I believe that was done here."

Jared put two men on the dismembered body and two men on Franklin after he told them exactly what had been done to that point. "We're going to process the other building. The first one done with their crime scene processes the house. I want a photograph of that note in the truck sent through CCS to me."

"Roger that, sir," Ray acknowledged, and his team split up without comment and went to work.

"Let's go, Bear."

Bear nodded and followed Jared to the office. Bear put cloth booties on his feet and new latex gloves on his hands. He followed Jared in and stared at the computers. The shed had no power, so they'd both been working on battery.

"Do you think Piper would know Christopher's password?"

Bear shrugged. "Probably. They were tight."

"Call her and see if she can provide it. Hit and hold the number four. That's Jewell's number."

Bear did as instructed and put the phone on

speaker. "Hey, Jared. How are things in Sedona?" Jewell asked.

"Hey, this is Bear. Can I talk to Piper?"

"Oh, sure. I have to black out my computers, so it'll take a hot minute, but hold on. Here's Zane."

"Did you find Franklin?"

He glanced over at Jared, who nodded his head. "Yeah. Dead. Things are not as they seemed."

Zane sighed. "They never are. Okay, we're sanitized. Hold on, Jewell is going to go get Piper."

A moment later, Piper's voice came through the line. "Hi, did you talk with Dr. Franklin?"

"No, we didn't get the chance. What does Christopher's personal computer look like?"

"A red laptop. He superglued a plate to the bottom of the computer with his telephone number on it."

Jared carefully picked up the laptop, and Bear leaned down and recited the number. "You found it?"

"We did. Do you know his password?"

Piper recited it, and Jared tapped it into the screen that lit up. "Thank you. I've got to go now, but I'll call as soon as possible."

"Are you safe?" Piper sounded worried.

"I am. Very safe. I'll talk with you soon." He disconnected and tossed the phone to Jared.

Jared pushed a button. "Con, can you access the computer I just turned on?"

"Is the Wi-Fi on?" Con asked. Bear heard the man typing in the background.

Jared looked down and tapped one of the function keys. "It is now. But I don't think there's a router anywhere near us."

Con laughed. "I have a satellite and the power of Guardian. As long as the Wi-Fi is on, I'm golden. Okay, I'm looking. There it is. Okay, shit. Not much battery life. You want this copied?"

"And secured. Locked down tight. Nobody knows what's being downloaded."

"Seventh level of hell," Con groaned. "It'll be a dash to the finish line, but I'll get most of it."

Jared stared at the pinned papers. "What in the hell is going on?"

Bear stood beside him. "Jared, I've been asking myself that since I arrived in Baton Rouge. I don't know, but I have a feeling this is a thread that will unravel way more than we bargained for."

Jared nodded. "I believe you could be correct."

CHAPTER 20

"Jared, the connection is secure, and you have the floor." Jason had already had the bullet point briefing, but the remainder of his family hadn't been filled in.

"Thank you. All right, over the last two months, Dom Ops has been working a case that has spilled over in a big way."

Joseph leaned forward. "You have my attention."

Jared shook his head. "I wish I didn't, Joseph. I wish I didn't. Here's the gist of what we know. Dr. Christopher Whitehead was a contractor with us in Cuba on our mission that brought the dirty bomb threat to an end."

"I remember that mission. We loaned them Smoke," Jacob said.

"And recruited Browning and Bear," Fury agreed.

Jared nodded. "Right, the same one. Dr. Whitehead was a nuclear physicist who once worked for the US government's Nuclear Program and consulted for the Nuclear Regulatory Commission."

"Was?" Joseph asked.

Jacob answered, "Tori told me he was killed, and his sister was somehow involved?"

"He was murdered in DC," Jared continued. "He was tortured, and his personal computer with his notes disappeared. At the time, we believed whoever killed him stole the computer. Whitehead's sister called Bear for help when she couldn't find him. During the following days, Dr. Whitehead's sister was shot at and almost run over. Whitehead's house was firebombed, ruining some of his work."

"Well, no offense intended, but whoever was after the sister was a rank amateur," Joseph grated out the words.

Jared lifted an eyebrow. "Thank God they were. She's the only one who can read Whitehead's notes. I had her and Bear come to DC to try to follow up on what her brother was doing. A John Doe was fished out of the Potomac the night they arrived. Piper Whitehead identified her brother's corpse. The next morning, three men killed one of my agents and critically wounded another who was in place to watch over her while Bear attended a meeting with Guardian. Bear killed all three of the hostiles and saved my agent's life. We vacated McGowen and Whitehead to Zane and Jewell's mountain. They're still there."

"All right. How does this affect any of us?" Joseph asked.

"We believed that Dr. Franklin, the person who Christopher Whitehead came to Washington to see, was involved with the declination of several Freedom of Information Act requests. Things that never should have been denied were categorically refused. Con, show them the video."

A video popped up on the screen. "This is Dr. Whitehead. Notice the bag," Jared said, and an arrow appeared on the screen.

"Okay, what about it?" Jacob leaned in as if he was trying to see it better.

Jared continued, "Notice how tight the strap is?"

"Yeah, it has some weight to it," Joseph added.

Jared spoke, "Now, here's Dr. Whitehead coming out of the building."

Jacob chuckled. "The damn thing is literally flapping in the wind."

"Right. We believe that Christopher Whitehead met with Dr. Franklin and gave the man his computer and research. We found Christopher's computer in a shed at a residence in the middle of nowhere which was owned by Dr. Franklin. We also found Dr. Franklin and the military member you see here." A photograph and an arrow showed up on the screen pinpointing the military member who was talking to Christopher Whitehead as he checked into the DIA. "Sergeant Phillips was hacked to death with an ax. Our doctors believe he was alive when it happened, based on the blood spatter and the wounds themselves."

"Franklin did that?" Joseph snorted. "Feisty for a professor."

"And completely impossible. Franklin had early-stage Parkinson's. He was going to retire at the end of the year because he was becoming increasingly unstable. According to his medical record, he was starting to have a problem with large motor skills."

"Which agency was he retiring from?" Jacob asked.

"Sorry, the DIA. On paper, he also worked as a consultant for the NSA and the NRC."

"On paper?" Jason leaned forward. That was a new development.

"Yes. Con, would you explain, please?"

"It's a straw house. There's paperwork with signatures showing he was a consulting member of both organizations. According to what I found, he worked remotely—never touching the facilities themselves. His only purpose, as far as we can see, was to monitor Freedom of Information Act requests. Very specific requests. Yet, Dr. Franklin never did the work."

"Who did?"

"Good question. Con?"

The man appeared on the screen. It wasn't the first time Jason had seen him. He chuckled internally because the man was the spitting image of Cary Grant. His mom had loved those old movies, and Con could have doubled for the guy. "When I was in the NSA, I signed a non-disclosure form."

Joseph snorted. "So, what? Dish, dude."

Con lifted an eyebrow. "Would you have the same cavalier attitude if I dished on Guardian?"

Joseph leaned forward, and the smile was not something Jason wanted to see again. "If you ever dished on Guardian, your throat would be slit, and your family would be mourning."

"Joseph," Jason growled his brother's name.

Con waved his hand in the air. "I know where my loyalties lie, and so does Guardian. That's why I'm now in violation of my NDA. When I was in the NSA, the research and development team completed a program that could access and delete specific items without any digital trail."

"Is that possible?" Jacob's question was Jason's, too.

"No, but they think it is," Jewell commented. "Con and I have reverse-processed this program. There's a ... What would you call it, Con?"

"A wake, maybe? Assume access was a boat and the wake was its trail in the digital platform. It's all water, but there's a disturbance in the water that you can only see for a short time."

"So, you can't detect it unless you see it happening?" Jason asked.

"Exactly." Jewell nodded. "We're developing a program to add to systems to sound an alarm if the effect happens, so we won't ever be hacked by the NSA. We're almost done."

"Okay, but let's get back to Franklin." Jason rerouted the conversation.

"Right," Jared continued, "The video you saw of Dr. Whitehead going into the DIA and coming back out was wiped from the system where Con retrieved it. We believe it was deleted with this program. Additionally, we believe, without verifiable proof, that the NSA and the NRC systems were hacked in the same way. Instead of deleting information, the hacker disapproved the requests as if they were coming from Dr. Franklin."

"And why do you believe Dr. Franklin didn't know about this?" Joseph leaned back in his chair and crossed his arms.

"We have a message from the grave," Jared said. "When we found Dr. Whitehead's personal computer, we also found Dr. Franklin's. When Dr. Whitehead left his office, Dr. Franklin called his supervisor and claimed he was ill. With his Parkinson's, it wasn't a stretch. He requested sick leave and drove from the DIA building to the airport, where he flew to Sedona. While in the air, Dr. Franklin wrote a lengthy document on his computer about his suspicions and concerns. He also annotated where Dr. Whitehead was correct in his assumptions about enriched uranium.

Although he was never able to finish his narrative, it appears we have one or more agencies in the United States covering up the movement and enrichment of uranium. All suspicions, but suspicions by two extremely intelligent people."

Jason leaned forward. "What organizations are involved at this point?"

"So far, the DIA and the NSA. We can assume the NRC because of the tie to Franklin that he knew nothing about," Jared responded. "I'd recommend we treat all agencies they are connected with or a parent of be considered suspect, too."

"I spoke to the Deputy Under Secretary of the DIA and told her of our concerns and our investigation." Jason swore, which he rarely did anymore. "I tipped our hand."

"We believe that could be true." Jared nodded in agreement.

"All right. What about Whitehead's sister?" Jacob asked.

"Good question. She's a good person and doesn't need to be caught up in this," Jewell added.

"That's another reason I wanted this meeting." Jared leaned toward the camera. "I want us to publicly drop everything. As far as anyone knows, the murder-suicide in Sedona was just that. Dr.

Whitehead's death was an accidental drowning, as initially reported, and his body was too beaten up from being in the water for an extended period to gather evidence. We put the information out through channels that can be monitored. I suggest we do the same for Dr. Franklin's death. As far as the public or anyone else in this agency is concerned, there's nothing to pursue. We get all eyes off Piper Whitehead and Bear McGowen. But …"

Jason cocked his head. "But what?"

"First, and I can't stress this enough, we can't trust anyone in the identified organizations, the DIA, NSA, and NRC. Everyone is a suspect."

Jason nodded. "I concur." He hated it, but it was necessary.

Jared seemed relieved. "Also, I think McGowen and Whitehead should be pulled toward the new headquarters facility. She has intimate knowledge of Christopher's work and can also help us decipher the information on Franklin's computer. The move gives them a fresh start, and McGowen is her protection."

"He's more than that." Zane chuckled.

Jason rubbed his chin. "Can we get her a

teaching position in Denver? That way, she's available to us but not constrained by us?"

Con responded, "Yeah, It's doable." He typed as he spoke. "There are three positions open in the greater Denver area."

"They'll both agree to this?" Jason asked.

"I think they will," Jewell answered.

Jason took off his glasses. "It'll take some time to spread the disinformation. Jewell, are you and Zane okay with more time with your guests?"

"Actually, we're more than okay with that." Jewell chuckled. "They cook, clean, and wear Dude out. I couldn't ask for better house guests."

"Then we have a plan. Jewell and Con, have we uncovered why the three men going after Ms. Whitehead were working together?"

Jewell answered. "Not a thing. Nothing in their past coincides—no work, service, prison time, or location."

"We're still working on it, sir," Con added. "There has to be some commonality. Three rando's don't just show up and start shooting."

"Any connection to any of the organizations in question?"

Both Con and Jewell shook their head. Jason

leaned back … "Try a *Strangers on a Train* approach."

"A what?"

"Huh?"

Jewell and Con asked at the same time.

Joseph sniggered. "You showed your age on that one, brother."

Jason rolled his eyes. "You're older and *grayer* than me, brother. The story goes something like this. Two entities swap murders. They both want a specific person dead, but to eliminate suspicion, they swap the murders. The murderer has no connection to the dead people but attacks them when they are the most vulnerable. The ones who want them dead have a solid alibi and allegedly no hand in the crime."

"Oh, that's wicked." Jewell's eyes got big, and she turned, talking to her husband off-screen, "Zane, we need to watch that movie."

"So, we look into what other agencies, or personnel in associated agencies, the murderers may have connections with." Con nodded. "Interesting way to look at it."

"Con, you want me to take that one?" Jewell asked her co-worker.

Con shook his head. "No, I'm the OPR for Jared. It's his case. I'll work it."

"If you need me, you know where I am," Jewell offered.

Jason put his glasses back on. "This brings up another point in this case. Con, Jewell, Zane, Jared, Jacob, Joseph, and I are the only ones who know about the suspicions Dr. Whitehead and Dr. Franklin had. As Jared knows, we've also been talking to Piper and Bear. She still thinks we are missing the bigger picture, the 'Solve for X' portion of the problem that Dr. Whitehead kept referencing. They want to continue to work with the data to see where it takes them. Of course, they won't make a move without informing us.

"We'll work on these issues without outside help. The smaller the trusted cadre in this situation, the better. No one is read in without my express permission. That goes for wives, brothers, sisters, parents, or anyone else. Does everyone understand?"

"Parents?" Con lifted an eyebrow. "I don't even want to know what you people's mom and dad do for a living." He shook his head.

"That includes Brando and Ring." Jason stared directly at their recruit from the NSA. His brother and cousin weren't cleared, and he wanted to ensure Con understood that point.

"I hear you loud and clear, sir," Con acknowledged.

"Zane. Talk to Bear and see if he and Piper are willing to relocate to Denver. Let me know what they decide. That's a short pole in the tent right now, but we need to work it so they can start living again when we have the ground level."

"Copy that, sir," Zane acknowledged the directive.

"Archangel out." Jason disconnected and leaned back in his chair. The only person he'd talked to was Anne Truman, the Undersecretary of Defense for Intelligence and Security. The call had been via secure coms.

She was either a damn good actor or didn't know what was happening in her house. He suspected the former rather than the latter. Most politicians could look you in the face and lie without a problem.

He drummed his fingers on his desk. The stakes were high. Higher than ever before. If any of their suspicions could be validated, it could skew the nation's trust. He glanced up at the flag across his office before picking up the phone and dialing the number he knew by heart but would never tell a soul.

"Gabriel."

He hated to pull his mentor in again, but there were some things that Gabriel needed to be briefed on, and this was one of them. "We have a situation."

CHAPTER 21

Bear worked with Piper on her kata. He'd been showing her the moves and helping her with her form while she'd been helping him gain stamina in running and the bedroom.

"No, shoulder's back, arm level, and sweep moving your left leg forward," he corrected her form, and she adjusted beautifully. He watched as she moved and fell into the movements with her. Dude was sleeping on the blue padded matt, but they didn't need all the room. The dog had grown in the nearly three months they'd been on top of the mountain, and their days had become routine. They worked with the data for most of the morning, then spent time running, perfecting their karate katas, sneaking in as much sex as humanly possible, keeping their hosts fed, and ensuring the household chores were done.

Piper had dropped out of the doctoral program and had given up her apartment. Guardian contracted movers had packed her out. Bear called his businesses twice a week and checked in. There were hiccups, but nothing his managers couldn't handle.

"Hey, got a minute?" Zane said from the doorway.

Bear popped out of his stance. "Keep going and watch the drop of your shoulder."

"Got it," Piper said as she continued to move through the kata.

Bear jogged over. "What's up?"

"Walk with me." Zane nodded toward the living room.

Bear frowned but walked with his host and friend. They went outside, and Zane took a deep breath of cool air. "Would you and Piper consider moving to the Denver area?"

Bear crossed his arms over his chest. "Why?"

"Guardian is making sure there are no eyes on you. It may take another month, but it's completely doable."

"Okay, and?" Bear waited for the next shoe to drop.

"We'd like Piper to be available to work on the data as she can. Our headquarters is now in Denver. There are three college-level positions up in that area that Piper could fill."

"As long as she's happy, I can open a gym anywhere." Bear rubbed the back of his neck. "Denver, huh?"

Zane nodded. "Yep."

"It would afford some good training opportunities."

"Sports all year round. Skiing, running, biking." Zane chuckled. "If you're into that type of thing."

Bear chuckled, "You know I am. World-class athletes train up there in mile-high air. I can see a market." Bear nodded. "I'll talk to Piper, but if Guardian wants it, we'll do it. You're probably ready to get rid of us."

"Actually, no. You guys take care of both of us, Dude, and the house. You can stay here permanently."

Bear laughed. "It's been good for a break, but Piper and I want to start our lives together."

"That sounds serious," Zane said, leaning against the mountain.

"We've spent every day of the last three months together. What we found early on has gotten stronger. I'll marry her one day."

"One day?" Zane chuckled. "Why not set a date?"

Bear grunted. "Piper has been working with Dr. Wheeler since she left the college. Her meds are on point, and Dr. Wheeler is great, but he also wants her to focus on herself now."

"I can see where that would be better for her but not for you." Zane sighed. "As long as you're protecting your woman and doing for her what you can, you aren't a detriment."

Bear nodded. He'd seen how Zane took care of Jewell. The woman was the center of his universe, and Bear could totally relate. Piper was the epicenter of everything in his life. All the rest could go to hell in a handbasket, and he wouldn't care as long as Piper was happy and healthy.

"Talk to her and get back to me. I'll see you at dinner."

"You got it," Bear said and leaned back against the wall, looking down the slope of the mountain. The trees were turning yellow and red. The chill in the air was a fore bearing of colder weather still to come. Sage's wedding was in three months, and he and Piper wanted to attend.

"What did Zane want?" Piper asked as Dude bolted past him to find his favorite stick, which happened to be the first one he could find.

"Guardian was wondering if we'd consider living in Denver."

Piper blinked up at him. "Denver?"

"There are teaching opportunities, and you'd still be able to work with the documents to try to solve for X." Bear put his arm over her shoulders. "I could build a gym that catered to world-class athletes who train in the region."

Piper turned to him and wrapped her arms around his waist. "I'd need to look at what jobs are open."

"Absolutely." Bear laughed at Dude, who'd treed a squirrel. The little fellow was chattering away at the massive animal that looked more like a wolf than a dog.

"We could get a dog," Piper suggested.

"A dog, yes. A mini-horse, no." Bear couldn't imagine a dog that size in a city or cooped up in a small yard. "But I think we'd need something else, too." He dropped for a kiss. The taste of the woman rocked his world.

She pulled away, and it took a moment for her eyes to open. He loved it when she did that. His inner caveman pounded his chest and grunted all the good sounds while dancing around the fire in victory. "What else would you want?"

"A promise that you'll marry me." Bear hadn't intended to ask, but Zane was right. He was good for her, and she was the best thing that had ever happened to him.

Piper stared up at him, and her smile spread across her face. "Are you sure you can handle all my baggage?"

"Load it up, baby. I'll handle anything you bring, anything you find along the way, and anything you may acquire in the future. I'm in it for the long haul."

"Oh, Mr. McGowen, you're sexy when you talk that way."

"Only when I talk?" He lifted his eyebrows a couple of times.

"Hmmm … no, not only when you talk. Why don't we go find a way to communicate without words."

He shook his head. "Not until you say yes."

Piper threw back her head and yelled, "Yes!"

Dude barked and started sprinting back to

where they stood. "As soon as we get tackled, we're going inside." Bear pushed her behind him and lowered to catch the monster flying in their direction. He grunted as the dog leaped into his arms, and his tongue lashed drool over Bear's face. Closing his eyes, he waited for the dog to wiggle to get down. When he did, he put the animal on his feet, and Piper petted him. The dog didn't spare her the kisses, but he didn't jump up on the woman. Thankfully, it was just Zane and him who ended up with that honor.

Bear laid on the bed, waiting for Piper to finish washing off Dude kisses. He watched her as she walked out of the bathroom, gloriously naked. Her long brown hair hung down to the small of her back, and her body was toned, tight, and all his. She kneed onto the bed, and he grabbed her, pulling her over him. She squealed and then settled, straddling him.

Leaning down, Piper kissed him. She'd started initiating sex more, and he was thrilled with how she blossomed into the person she was always meant to be. A strong, intelligent, sexy, independent woman. She didn't need him to protect her or watch over her, but he'd always be there to do just that. She didn't need him to love her, but he'd love her until the day he died. Probably beyond.

She lifted, and he cupped her cheek. "I love you."

"I love you, too."

They'd confessed their love to each other weeks ago, but the words were still magical. He prayed they always would be. Bear rolled her under him. He wanted to taste every part of her and make her shiver in anticipation. Piper was a sensual woman, and the way she arched into his touch and the sounds she made when she was aroused were the sexiest things he'd ever experienced.

He entered her gently, moving slowly. Piper arched under him and ran her hands up his arms, gripping his shoulders. He watched a rose hue of blush start at her breasts and work its way up to her cheeks. The abandon with which she responded was mesmerizing and erotic as hell.

Bear felt her tighten, and he sped up, driving harder as she finished. He sat up and pulled her up on his lap, still on his cock. Piper grabbed his shoulders, and he held her up about four inches. He drove his hips up into her, and she gasped, "Yes!"

Bear lost all sense of anything but the two of

them together. Piper opened her eyes and stared down at him as he climaxed. That look, the one that held love and trust and forever in her eyes, was the most beautiful thing he'd ever experienced. And it was his for the rest of his life.

One month later:

Anne Truman leaned back in the private lounge's best chair and looked down at the red sole of her Louboutin shoe before speaking. "The debacle is fixed and complete. Whitehead is dead. He gave us everything. His sister could read his notes, but she had no idea what he was working on. We have it on excellent authority that the knee-jerk reaction at the hotel was unnecessary." The Undersecretary of Defense for Intelligence and Security sighed and looked at her nails. They needed a polish change. She sipped her champagne cocktail and continued, "The documents were destroyed. It was necessary to eliminate Franklin and Sergeant Phillips. There are no loose ends. The locals uncovered the murder-suicide two days ago. Everything indicates that they're closing the case as exactly that. Our teams were very adept at their jobs. There's nothing to be concerned about."

"Untrue." Charles Cahill, her contemporary from the NSA, leaned forward. "We have a loose end."

Anne Truman cocked her head. "We do not. If there's a loose end, it hasn't been disclosed." She uncrossed her legs, sweeping her legs gracefully to the side. She watched as the men followed her motion with their eyes. She'd smirk at the old fools, but that would let them know her disdain for them. "Do tell, Charles, what end is loose?"

The man swallowed hard. "The program used to wipe out the films across from the DIA facility was one of ours."

Anne failed to see the problem. "You said it was untraceable."

"It is. It's one of a kind."

"So, what's the problem?" Anne set her warm champagne cocktail on the table.

"We lost one of our programmers to Guardian. He'd know it was us."

Anne leaned back in her chair. "Has anyone received any intel that Guardian was suspicious?

That the carefully constructed murder-suicide crime scene hadn't worked?"

Four heads went east and west. Anne would have furrowed her brow if her dermatologist hadn't used so much damn Botox at last week's appointment. "Has anyone had any indication that Guardian is suspicious about Dr. Whitehead's death?" Again, there was no verbal answer. Anne narrowed her eyes at Charles. "This programmer you mentioned. It would be unfortunate if he had an accident."

The man leaned forward, and his eyes flitted to the door, which was shut. "It's not that simple. He's fallen off the map. I had my people try to find him. Nothing. No digital footprint since the day he left the NSA."

"Guardian surely has records." She waved her hand dismissively.

"My best can't get through Guardian's firewalls; if they tried, Guardian would know where the attack was coming from."

"Not if you used the program with which you wiped out the video feeds. He's your loose end, Charles. Figure out a way, and we'll populate an unassociated hit team." Earl Gainer, the Undersecretary of the National Geospatial-Intelligence

Agency, murmured. "Ones who are better trained than last time. I hope."

"We didn't expect resistance. The Guardian stationed nearby took all three out, but he was direly injured in the process." Glenn Montage, Deputy Director of the National Reconnaissance Office, sipped his single malt after he spoke. "But that situation in its totality is a non-player now. We've removed any irritation and those that remain can't harm us."

Anne nodded. "And Guardian?" She turned to look at her counterpart in the Defense Counterintelligence and Security Agency.

Jay Horne adjusted his glasses, as was his way before he spoke. "I've talked at length with Jared King. The agency is gathering the shreds of its past and moving forward. They have no interest in any of the cases and haven't indicated that they suspect anything."

"Is that common? Letting go of an investigation?" Anne pressed the man.

"No, but the times are uncommon for Guardian. They're in tatters except for Domestic Operations, and from what I can tell, they're focusing on high-value assets and cases. They've moved their corporate headquarters to Denver. I think they're removing the emphasis from their overseas operations." Jay adjusted his glasses again. The habit was annoying as hell. "My field operatives have told me they haven't seen any Guardian operatives overseas except a couple of teams that tend to operate perpetually in Mongolia, which of course, gives them access to Russia, China, and other countries that we will not irritate with our presence."

"Keep an eye on them. We've worked far too hard and for too long to have this all blow up in our faces now." Anne smoothed her hair and crossed her legs again. "Guardian may be down, but they aren't out. The CIA and FBI are well-trained and won't make quick turns because the bureaucracy won't allow it. Guardian can spin at the drop of a dime." She stared at each man in turn. "Do not drop your guard. We are within our timetable, but we can't afford any more situations as we had with Whitehead. Am I clear?"

Each man nodded as she turned and focused on them. Anne reached to the side table and pressed the buzzer ending their meeting. The men talked among themselves about droll and boring political speculation as the waiters entered the room with fresh drinks for each of them. Nothing in Washington was done in offices.

"Ms. Truman, your car is outside."

"Thank you." She sipped her drink and set it down on the table. "Gentlemen, it was a delight to run into you." She stood and made her way to the limo waiting out front.

"Where to, ma'am?"

"The White House." She sat back and smiled. One day, she'd be there as president.

EPILOGUE

The kill shot was never hard for Billy to take. There wasn't any morbid sense of dread or issues with morality. He was a sniper. He shot at his targets and rarely missed his mark. He had no family. Hell, according to every known record, he was dead. Long ago, buried and forgotten by all he used to know. He'd worked for animals, and thankfully he'd been afforded an opportunity to switch sides. Not many were. He was lucky because he knew someone who was also supposed to be dead. Small world. Smaller when you're a shooter as skilled as he'd become.

The helicopter made the shot harder. Not impossible, but harder. He'd had the bird in his sights and was waiting for the command to kill the shooter or the pilot. It didn't matter which. He could easily make the transfer.

This mission was unexpected, and he'd been flying for almost eighteen hours, both in planes and helicopters, before he made the trek on foot to his current location. He'd slept when he could. A survival tactic he'd learned early in his military career. The damn Marines had that right. Never stand when you can sit, never sit when you can lie down, and never stay awake when you can sleep.

His earpiece was silent, but he knew it worked, and he was a patient man. He excelled in waiting. There was gunfire in the compound below him. The helicopter made another large circle in a holding pattern. He led the aircraft with his rifle. It would take time for the bullet to travel and so he moved the sight picture on the scope to where he anticipated the aircraft to turn. A twitch of a smile kicked the corner of his lip up. The pilot was predictable.

"Cobra One, status."

"Still in position. Locked on target." He watched the door of the helicopter open, and the gunner slid out, suspended by a sling so he wouldn't fall.

"Guardian, shooter on the rail." He focused on the shooter and flipped his weapon off safe.

"Cobra One, delete the threat."

He nestled his cheek against the stock of the weapon. "Gunner or bird?"

"Both."

"Confirm bird and gunner." He rattled off the request as he adjusted behind the weapon and settled.

"Confirming both bird and gunner."

"Roger that."

He watched as the gunner went through the movements of charging his high-powered machine gun. He exhaled and held his breath when his lungs were halfway full. A practiced move he'd done so many times that it was second nature. The squeeze on the trigger was also routine. Soft, measured, no jerk and precise. Just the way he'd trained. The bullet left his rifle. With conservation of motion, he swung his highly personalized Barrett M-82 and found his next target. The pilot jerked the helicopter's holding pattern, probably from the shock of the bullet. The aircraft veered right, flowing downward and to the right. Billy accounted for the wind and led the machine. He pulled the trigger and watched his target. The helicopter's windshield shattered, preventing him from seeing if he eliminated the target. The helicopter funneled into a downward spin. Billy lifted his gaze from the scope and watched as the helicopter dropped onto the ground and fire erupted in a massive ball that plumed upward, sucking up smoke and debris into the vacuum the fire eating up the oxygen caused. Another explosion vibrated the air, and the twisted metal of the aircraft landed for a second time. There was no way anyone survived the crash, but Billy would make sure.

"Guardian, I have eliminated gunner. Bird is down. Moving in to confirm." He held his position, listening to random pops of gunfire from the compound.

"Hold Cobra One."

"Copy." He knew the other components of the mission were still working. Billy kept his eyes open and waited. He wasn't a fool. He may be dead as far as the world was concerned, but he would not do something stupid and make his cover a fact. Besides, there was someone he wanted to see again. A sweet thing. She was all fire and vinegar, and that red hair was a warning sign. But then again, he'd never paid much attention to warning signs.

"Cobra One, move in."

"Copy." Billy slung his Barrett and grabbed his M-4. In close, the M-4 was easier to handle. He'd validate his kill and then head to the extraction point. Then he'd make his way back to South Dakota and then maybe take a chance with that spitfire of a woman. After all, even dead men could have dreams.

ALSO BY KRIS MICHAELS

Kings of the Guardian Series

Jacob: Kings of the Guardian Book 1

Joseph: Kings of the Guardian Book 2

Adam: Kings of the Guardian Book 3

Jason: Kings of the Guardian Book 4

Jared: Kings of the Guardian Book 5

Jasmine: Kings of the Guardian Book 6

Chief: The Kings of Guardian Book 7

Jewell: Kings of the Guardian Book 8

Jade: Kings of the Guardian Book 9

Justin: Kings of the Guardian Book 10

Christmas with the Kings

Drake: Kings of the Guardian Book 11

Dixon: Kings of the Guardian Book 12

Passages: The Kings of Guardian Book 13

Promises: The Kings of Guardian Book 14

The Siege: Book One, The Kings of Guardian Book 15

The Siege: Book Two, The Kings of Guardian Book 16

A Backwater Blessing: A Kings of Guardian Crossover

Novella

Montana Guardian: A Kings of Guardian Novella

Guardian Defenders Series

Gabriel

Maliki

John

Jeremiah

Frank

Creed

Sage

Bear

Guardian Security Shadow World

Anubis (Guardian Shadow World Book 1)

Asp (Guardian Shadow World Book 2)

Lycos (Guardian Shadow World Book 3)

Thanatos (Guardian Shadow World Book 4)

Tempest (Guardian Shadow World Book 5)

Smoke (Guardian Shadow World Book 6)

Reaper (Guardian Shadow World Book 7)

Phoenix (Guardian Shadow World Book 8)

Valkyrie (Guardian Shadow World Book 9)

Flack (Guardian Shadow World Book 10)

Ice (Guardian Shadow World Book 11)

Hollister (A Guardian Crossover Series)

Andrew (Hollister-Book 1)

Zeke (Hollister-Book 2)

Declan (Hollister- Book 3)

Hope City

Hope City - Brock

HOPE CITY - Brody- Book 3

Hope City - Ryker - Book 5

Hope City - Killian - Book 8

Hope City - Blayze - Book 10

The Long Road Home

Season One:

My Heart's Home

Season Two:

Searching for Home (A Hollister-Guardian Crossover Novel)

Season Three:

A Home for Love

STAND ALONE NOVELS

A Heart's Desire - Stand Alone

Hot SEAL, Single Malt (SEALs in Paradise)

Hot SEAL, Savannah Nights (SEALs in Paradise)

Hot SEAL, Silent Knight (SEALs in Paradise)

ABOUT THE AUTHOR

Wall Street Journal and USA Today Bestselling Author, Kris Michaels is the alter ego of a happily married wife and mother. She writes romance, usually with characters from military and law enforcement backgrounds.

Printed in Great Britain
by Amazon

25707834R00176